KT-362-833

CONTENTS

INTRODUCTION

I only really became properly aware of World War One when I went into the sixth form of my south London grammar school, way back in the early 1970s. I had chosen to do English Literature as one of my three A levels, and found myself studying the poetry of Wilfred Owen. I was soon totally gripped by his work, the tiny number of beautifully written, deeply felt poems about his experiences as a young officer that he had managed to complete before he was killed in action a week before the war ended.

Reading them made me want to find out more about him, and about the war itself. So I read whatever I could find – the poems of Siegfried Sassoon, for example, and the great memoirs of the war, including Sassoon's own *Memoirs of an Infantry Officer*, and *Goodbye to All That* by Robert Graves, both of whom knew Owen.

I read lots of history books too, and learned what a wasteful conflict the war had been. It began in 1914 and lasted over four years, during which eight and a half million soldiers died, almost one million of them from Britain and its then empire. There was fighting in many parts of the world, but it was the horror of trench warfare in France and Belgium that captured my imagination – the slaughter of thousands of young men for a few yards of bomb-blasted mud.

After a while I began to realise that I'd known about the war all along, but hadn't taken much notice of it. In the entrance hall of my school there was a board bearing the names of former pupils who had died in the war, and it was quite a list. There was a local war memorial too, a tall obelisk of white stone with a much longer list of names carved on it. Every year on the nearest Sunday to 11th November – the day on which the war ended in 1918 – wreaths were placed around the memorial. And whenever 11th November itself fell on a weekday, we would have a special school assembly with a full two-minute silence, so we could remember 'those who had given their lives for their country'.

From then on, I noticed war memorials in many places. I played rugby for my school, and saw memorials in the entrance halls of the schools we visited. There were memorials in other London suburbs, on the sides of office buildings and factories, in stations and in parks. Many were similar white obelisks, but some were big and dramatic and included statues of soldiers. In later years, I discovered that there are memorials everywhere in these islands – in every village and town and suburb, in the centre of every city. It is almost as if a silent army of ghosts haunts the land which they left and never returned to in life. But with so many dead in such a short time, how could it be otherwise?

Of course, when I first started reading Wilfred Owen's poetry, many of the soldiers who had fought in the war were still alive, elderly men in their seventies and eighties. They have all gone now, but most families still have stories about great-grandfathers who fought in the trenches, great-uncles who were killed, others who returned maimed or disabled for life, either physically or mentally. World War One – or as it was called at the time, *The Great War* – runs like a scar through all of us. In many ways it made this country what it is today, and that is why we should always remember it. That's the point of all the war memorials, of all the Remembrance Day services, of all those poppies we buy.

Yet for me the best way to remember the war is through the words of writers. This is something Wilfred Owen himself recognised. He wrote that 'true poets must be truthful', and by this I think he meant that the truth of what happened is to be found in the poems and stories written about it. That's where you'll find an understanding of the impact of the war on the people who lived through it, and who came after. And that's why I came up with the idea for this anthology of short stories. I thought there couldn't be a better way for today's young readers to find out about the war than by putting a collection of great stories in your hands, especially as the anthology is being published in this centenary year.

I wanted this book to cover as wide a range as possible, which is why you'll find stories set in very different places. There are stories about young men in the trenches, of course, but also about the people they left behind, and about what happened to them and their families because of their experiences. There are stories about the impact of the war on children, in this country and in France and Belgium and Germany. There are stories about soldiers from Britain's empire who fought in the war – about young men from Ireland, India and Australia. There is sadness and pain and suffering in these stories, but there is hope too, and I have a feeling that if Wilfred Owen himself could read them, he would approve.

I like to think so, anyway.

Tony Bradman

THE MAN IN THE RED TROUSERS
JAMILA GAVIN

Author's note:

I very much wanted to reflect the participation of Indian soldiers in World War One and during my research came across Khudadad Khan, the first Indian soldier to be awarded the Victoria Cross for bravery. Even more poignant was that by belonging to the Duke of Connaught's 129th Baluchi Regiment, his uniform was so incongruous for the muddy battlefields of Europe with their bright green turbans and jackets, and conspicuous bright red trousers. I didn't look any further. A story was already forming in my mind before the research was over.

My name's Lotte Becke. I hope you'll remember me if all this ends badly. You see, I'm Flemish and I live in Flanders, though you would call it Belgium, but don't let Uncle Henrik hear you.

We're at war with Germany. I don't know why. I'll be ten next month. My sister's called Els, she's only five.

We're sitting in the back of the cart, our legs dangling, our backs hard up against a mountain of our possessions: tables, chairs, clothes, bedding, cutlery, everything we could pile onto the cart pulled by our farm horse, dear Nellie, who was too old and bedraggled to have been taken off to be a war horse. Old Henrik had come banging on our door, his voice panting and gasping as if he would have a heart attack. 'Leave, leave – NOW,' and Mother told Els and me to get out the cart and harness up Nellie, while she flew round grabbing at anything and everything, hurling it up onto the back of the cart. I heard her weeping and muttering, 'Oh, I can't leave this, I must have that, this belonged to Grandma, and this was your father's favourite plate. Oh, where is your father?'

Where was Dad? So many people had fled. Uncle

Henrik said Belgium wasn't meant to be on anyone's side. He said we were neutral, but that meant nothing. Kaiser Bill's troops walked in anyway and, within a month, had occupied our country without so much as a by your leave. There wasn't much our little army could do against the might of the Germans – though we gave them a run for their money, but half our village have left, looking for refuge in England, France or Holland.

Mum wouldn't go. 'Cowards,' she cried. When Dad's army unit was scattered, he went to join the resistance, helping the French. 'If more men had been like him, we wouldn't be running like rats,' she cried.

All this time Mum had stayed put, refusing to leave, even as we heard the guns and shells getting nearer, and more of the village fled. 'Your father may come home. I can't have him coming back to an empty house, and no food on the table.'

Food. What food? Every evening, ever since the fighting got nearer and nearer to us, Els and I had scrambled into the turnip and potato fields with sacks, scrabbling in the muddy furrows for anything we could find. Poor Farmer Bodiecke, what could he do? Then he ran too, abandoning his crops, so we felt they were ours for the taking. It wasn't just us; there were others. I saw Michael a little further away.

He was in my class at school – when there was a school. It was hit by the bombardment, and set on fire because some soldiers had been sheltering there, so it doesn't exist now. None of us caught each other's eye; all of us ashamed as we stole from our neighbours. But we couldn't starve, could we? At first we didn't need to steal; Father Bernard from the church got everyone to contribute wheat, potatoes, turnips, carrots – anything they could to build up a store so that food could be distributed fairly. There was always a line of us queuing up for our ration. But then…

On 28th October 1914, British intelligence intercepts German radio traffic. Germans preparing to attack near Hollebeke at 05:30 on 29th October. Aerial reconnaissance spots German transport columns on the move.

I was up my tree. I can see Hollebeke from here. It's our nearest town and I saw them coming. Mama hates it when I climb trees. She says it's unladylike. But this is my secret tree, and it's where I climb to get some peace from everyone, and I can think. Everything's bad at the moment with this war, and Mama is so nervous and irritable. Well, everyone is. So there I was, up at the top of my tree, and I saw them emerging out of the misty horizon: an army – like a great, never-ending river – coming towards us. I saw them with my own eyes.

Of course, I slid down my tree so fast I grazed my knees and arms, but I had to tell Mama and Uncle Henrik.

'This is bad,' muttered old Uncle Henrik. 'And it's going to get worse. We've got to leave, Marta. They're coming here.'

'No, no!' My mother wouldn't hear of it. 'Why would they want to come to our village?' And she went back to fiercely scrubbing some muddy turnips, as if she could scrub out her fears and the sounds of war we'd put up with for days and days.

'It's bad,' old Henrik repeated. 'They'll come. Things will get worse.'

Could it get any worse? The Germans, French and British had already been fighting ferociously in all the woods and ditches and trenches around us. The noise was so terrible, I thought our brains would burst, or the sky would crack, and all the time it was the screams and moans of wounded and dying soldiers which never seemed to go away.

The Germans want to get to Ieper. That's a town not far from here near the border with France, and they call it Ypres. The British and Belgians are fighting tooth and nail to stop them, but the Germans are desperate; their plan is to overcome the coastal ports in Belgium and France and conquer France. That's what old Henrik said, and there's nothing he doesn't know. It all sounded like one of our board games; snakes and ladders. But we knew it wasn't. Somehow, our village is becoming the centre of a life and death battle; Gheluvelt. Have you heard of it? It's near Hollebeke, not far from Ieper/Ypres. We're only small, and very insignificant, but old Henrik was sure they would come to our village because we were high – well, high for round here where everywhere else is flat as a pancake. We're on a kind of ridge, overlooking the Menin to Ypres Road in both directions.

'What will happen if the Germans get Ieper?' I asked.

'For goodness sake, Lotte,' snapped my mother, 'questions, questions! Get out of my hair. Take your little sister and amuse her. We have so much to do.'

So I grabbed Els's hand. She didn't want to come, and began struggling and crying. 'I'll show you a secret if you'll shut up!' I hissed at her. So she shut up, and I dragged her along a winding path through the deep undergrowth, till we reached my tree. You see how dire things had become for me to show my little sister my most treasured secret?

I made her sit at the bottom, while I leaped for the over-hanging branch, and swung myself up.

'Lotte!' gasped Els. 'You're not allowed to climb trees. What will Mama say?'

'Nothing,' I snapped, 'if you don't tell on me.' I climbed higher and higher.

'Can I come up?' Els shrieked.

'No! You're too little.'

'What can you see?'

Below me, the army came relentlessly closer; above, the sky hung grey, watery, merciless, as if heaven itself had closed its doors. Not even birds seemed to want to fly across its impenetrable face.

'I can see thousands of soldiers,' I cried. 'Men pushing cannons on wheels, horses, poor horses, struggling to pull machine guns, churning up the mud, soldiers on bicycles – hundreds of them, and trucks, platoons of foot soldiers, men with guns, bayonets and grenades.'

'Lotte, it's raining,' my sister wailed.

Yes, it was raining; again. And soon the army looked like a vast population of ghosts advancing through swishing curtains of rain.

'We'd better go to the barn,' I said, slithering down again. I had a deep knotted fear in my stomach.

'I'm hungry,' she whined.

'So am I,' I retorted, running ahead of her to the

barn. When we got there, we found Michael huddled in a corner.

'Why don't you go home, Michael?' I asked rather fiercely, like a cat defending its territory. I suppose I didn't sound too kind. He had never been a friend of mine. In fact, he had no friends, and the other children liked to tease him dreadfully for his red hair, and for being a Walloon. We Flemish don't much like Walloons round here. I mean, in Flanders we speak Dutch and they speak French. Anyway, he didn't seem to have a father but only a mother who was so poor he often came to school without any shoes.

Michael didn't move. Then I saw he was crying. It's the sort of crying when your face doesn't crumple up. He just stared at me, with the tears rolling down his blank face.

'I've got a turnip,' I said, digging into the pocket of my smock. 'Do you want it?'

He nodded wildly, and almost snatched the small, muddy turnip from my hand. Els and I watched in silence, as he gobbled it up mud and all, as if he hadn't eaten in days, and all the time we could hear the rain outside coming down in a steady roar. Then I pulled out another turnip and gave it to Els. 'Leave some for me,' I said.

It had been exciting at first; war. Last July, in full

summer, when war was declared, we'd been helping with the harvesting, when suddenly all the men of our village put on uniforms and went off to fight; Dad too. I would have gone if I'd been a boy, and older. But I had to stay with my mother and all the other women and children and old men, to keep the farms running. The weeks went by; the war got closer, and we heard most of our army had already been smashed. Where was Dad? Old Uncle Henrik and my mother argued dreadfully. He said we should leave, but she wouldn't.

Autumn arrived, and so did the rain. The Germans came up the road like fire-spitting dragons, and the French and British troops piled in to stop them. Shells and mortars from both sides crashed all around us. The noise made my heart shake and my ears shudder. Worst was when I went into the village to get food, and a mortar fell right into the bread queue. I saw my first dead bodies close up. That day, I felt fear.

'But why, Uncle Henrik?' I asked. 'Why do they want war?'

'Why, why!' my mother shouted irritably, holding her head. 'Why is the world round? Stop asking silly questions, Lotte.'

Old Henrik put a sympathetic arm round me. 'It's her nerves, Lotte,' he soothed. 'You see, it's like this...' He almost sang out the situation:

'The Germans hate the Russians,

and Russians love the Serbs,

and the Serbs hate the Germans,

but the Austrians love the Germans,

and the English love the French,

and the French don't love the Russians

but decided to make friends with them,

and any friend of the Russians is an enemy of the Germans.

'So when the Austrian Prince Ferdinand was assassinated in Serbia, the Germans thought this the perfect excuse to go to war against Serbia as they had to defend their friends, the Austrians;

'and the Serbs are friends with Russia,

and Russia would be forced to fight on their side,

and the French would have to side with Russia,

and the English would have to side with France,

and all the allies promised to protect us – Belgium –

and...and...and...'

Uncle ran out of breath and sighed as he used his finger to draw up the lines. 'See, Lotte, that's how small wars become world wars. Let it be a lesson.' He might have added, 'If you survive.'

But my head was spinning and I couldn't

remember who was friends with who. All I knew was that in our country the Flemish hated the Walloons. 'And what about us, Uncle Henrik, who's friends with us?' I wailed.

It was the morning of 29th October 1914. Henrik came yelling and shouting, his voice almost soprano in panic. 'We've got to go!' It was raining so hard, it thudded into the ground like bullets.

It had been raining for days. When there was a lull the woods dripped, as if trying to rid themselves of the weight of autumn rain. The fields were waterlogged, and we always came back from foraging in the fields all muddied from our eyebrows to our toes. Today, we hadn't even had time to scrub off when we fled our house. We could hear the boom of cannons, and shells whistling through the air, and there was the constant rat-a-tat-tat of rifles. At last Mother agreed.

So here we are: my mother is up front driving our farm horse, Uncle Henrik's sitting next to her, and Els and me are at the back, clutching our dog, Loki, between us. I hear mother flip the reins and urge Nel forwards when there is a whistling, and a bang. All hell breaks loose. I don't know how to describe it. We had nearly reached the end of our lane to join others on the Menin Road; one minute there was just the creaking of cart wheels and horses and children's voices and babies crying, and the next it was like all heaven and earth collided.

Explosions: whistling, whining, sizzling. People running; screaming; then there is one big bang right under our cart.

My mother flies through the air, her arms outstretched, as if suddenly she has become a bird, and Els and I find ourselves in the road, I don't know how. Perhaps we flew too, but I'm all huddled up on top of my sister, cradling her head next to mine; deafened, blinded, and in such shock we don't cry, or scream. I feel nothing; no sensation inside or out. We crouch together; I don't know how long. Finally, I raise my head. My mouth is open but no sound comes out. It's as though my eyes hold all the terror to themselves; that scene of devastation around us. Then I blink, I breathe, I howl; such a howl, that Els flings herself into my lap crying, 'Mummy, Mummy! I want Mummy.'

I see Uncle Henrik. He is dead. I won't tell you how I know; so is our horse, Nel. And there are lots of other dead bodies and animals around. Perhaps Loki's dead too. I can't see her. I can't see my mother. I whimper once. 'Mama!' I wonder if she's been blown into another country; and us too. I have known this street all my life; I was born in this village; been to school here and know everybody; but at that moment, I think, we too are dead and gone to hell. I can't recognise anyone or anything. I can't even see how to get back to our house.

But then I look up, and there through the swirling grey of smoke and rainy sky, I see my tall brave tree; my secret tree. How strange that the mortars and bombs and shells had raked through the undergrowth and flattened all the shrubs, yet not touched my tree. There she stands for everyone to see; a secret no longer, glistening with raindrops, like a beacon, its leaves brown and orange in the watery autumn light. Although it is scorched and disfigured, I recognised my tree by the red-spotted handkerchief which I'd tied to an upper branch just to claim it as mine. Now I know where I am.

I lift Els to her feet and kiss her. 'Let's go home,' I say, taking her hand. Perhaps Mummy will be there.

She wasn't. But Michael was.

* * *

A Soldier of the British Empire

Don't go, don't go.
Stay back, my friend.
Crazy people are packing up,

THE MAN IN THE RED TROUSERS

Flowers are withering and friendships are breaking.
Stay back, my friend.
Allah gives bread and work,
You wouldn't find soothing shades anywhere else.
Don't go, my friend, don't go.

They sang this song in my village the night before I left, and I hum it now as I crouch behind my machine gun.

I am Khudadad Khan, a sepoy in the Duke of Connaught's 129th Own Baluchis Infantry Regiment. We were among 20,000 other Indian soldiers, most of them – poor shivering devils – wearing thin khaki uniforms more suited to the heat of the desert than these bitterly cold, wet, sodden fields. But you can't miss us in our red trousers and white boots – at least they were white when we disembarked from our ship in Marseilles, and they put us on a train across France to this hell in some country called Belgium. I'd never heard of Belgium till they brought us here.

I was still smart in my rifle-green jacket with red piping and silver buttons, and matching green turban with the regimental badge on the front. But now, after we've had a few days of crawling through trenches and digging in, you can barely tell the difference. We're all the colour of mud. I suppose it means we're better camouflaged.

I look at my friend, Mohammed; he too looks like some clay creature, born out of the earth. Just his eyes gleaming like bright stars, the only two points of light in this murky world of water, mud and gloom. We've known each other ever since we joined the army, and have become friends. But now, in just over a week, thrown together into this hell they call Flanders, watching our comrades suffer and die, we are brothers. He is closer to me than my own mother. Every time we go over the top and land in another trench, I look for his bright eyes.

It had been raining when we disembarked after weeks at sea all the way from India. It is still raining. Oh, Mother India. I shut my eyes and see my village and my family, and our plots of barley and lentils, and fields of wheat; a flat landscape, not so different from here, yet the difference between paradise and hell. *Don't go, my friend, don't go.* We had no time to adjust, but we were rushed into action. The Germans' relentless march towards the French ports had to be stopped, our officers told us. 'We must first stop them getting to Wipers.' *Wipers* – that's what the Tommies called Ypres. So we all set off for Wipers, but we only got as far as Hollebeke where the Germans had already dug in.

Are we fighting for this? There's no city here, no palaces or forts. Just churned-up earth and, where once there were green fields are now oceans of mud; and woods, no longer woods but trees, stripped down to charred stumps sticking up through the ground like bad teeth. *Flowers are withering* – I still have the small garland of the flowers they draped round my neck when I left. They're pressed against my chest. I smelled their perfume for days, but now, yes, they have browned, though I force my nose into the withered petals to remember their perfume so that I don't retch with the stink of rotting corpses of dead soldiers and horses. And nothing stops me dropping to my knees to face Mecca and saying my prayers.

Allahu Akbar,
Ash-ahdu-an-la-ilaha-illahah.

I feel Allah on my side, especially when once, as I dropped to my knees, I heard the searing hot whistle of a shell which skimmed my head, but my comrade next to me fell face down with half his head blown off. Please, not my friend; not Mohammed. I choke back a sob. A brown shape rises from the ground. Eyes gleam towards me through the mud and blood. It's Mohammed. Thank God. Please, Allah, protect my brother.

We fight – oh, how we fight, though only Allah knows what we are fighting for; our machine guns rattle away as we pan across the enemy foot soldiers and cut them down. But ours too – I saw the 1st Gloucesters, bayonets fixed and staring rigidly in front, racing forward, then falling, falling, falling – like sheaths of corn under the scythe. Out of eighty lads, only thirteen make it through. So they bring in more brigades: the Worcesters, the Gordons, the Welsh Guards, the Fourth Middlesex, the Indian brigades – us – and none of us really believe we'll fare any better. We know we too will be cut down.

It's still raining. Not like the welcome monsoon rain of home, nor the soft winter rain we get later, which is so wondrous for our crops. No, this is a mean rain, a nipping, stinging rain like vengeful hornets; a rain which fills up the furrows and shell holes, turning dugouts into lakes and fields into a hell of sucking, squelching, immobilising mud; a rain which dilutes the rivulets of blood gushing into the ditches, and dilutes the spirit in one's guts. And, along with the swish and squelch of rain and mud, I hear the ceaseless dirges of the wounded and dying.

My name is Khudadad Khan. I hope you'll remember me if all this ends badly. My friend is Mohammed. We are machine-gunners. My regiment has hunkered down near the town of Hollebeke. The Germans have come too; wave after wave in a massive onslaught, everyone fighting to gain possession of the Menin Road to Ypres. Shafts of Germans advance from various directions to try and penetrate the British defences like arrows. I glimpse my fellow Indians: those Sikhs fight like tigers, but even they go down never to rise again; more of them fall, and more and more. They are cutting us to ribbons, and the screams of the dying lacerate the air. German reconnaissance balloons float above. How beautiful. We aim our rifles at them and fire. Useless.

* * *

Els said she saw a man in red trousers. She had gone out in the night to pee.

I told her she was dreaming.

'No, no! He was...' She can't remember what he was, and now she is asleep before she even finishes her sentence,

Anyway, how could she have seen anything in the dark?

I'm awake now. We are all sleeping in the kitchen. It's warmer there. I manage to keep the fire going. Michael helps me. He never went away, and if the truth be known, I was glad to have him stay. He said his house was flattened, and he didn't know where his mother was. We've brought down all the blankets and snuggle next to each other for extra warmth. Michael is curled up in a tight ball as if not yet born,

Els moans, 'Mummy! I'm hungry.'

I've got to get food. I creep out of our house, looking all around me. I know there are soldiers everywhere, and I have no idea who are good and who are bad. I have to be careful. If the German soldiers decided to come to our house, I don't know what they'd do to us. We've heard terrible stories, even how they eat babies.

I'm heading for my tree. I need to see if it is safe to get into the fields and pick some turnips – if there are any under all that mud. I've always said I could find my way around, blindfolded, and I prove it as I move like a silent shadow through the dark without stumbling or bumping into anything. I get there, and stand embracing the trunk, pressing my face into its rippling bark as though it were my mother. Then I start to climb, feeling for every branch and foothold. Up and up. I know where my vantage point is; that fork between two thin branches near the top. My eyes are wide open, but I can't see a thing in the darkness, so I just shuffle into position and wait. I know from which direction the dawn will come.

On 29th October 1914 the German Army Group Fabeck are ordered to take Gheluvelt. There are five divisions and two hundred and sixty six heavy guns. They move

through the night to be ready to attack the next
morning 30th October.

Through the darkness, I see faint lights bobbing, like
fireflies. As I watch, daylight is now thrusting
through the night like a swimmer trying desperately
to reach the surface, all wet and pale. I'm gripped by
a sudden terror. How could I forget? It's autumn
and half the tree's leaves have been stripped away.
Anyone looking up can easily see me. I must get
down before it gets too light; but suddenly I freeze.
I see now what those fireflies were: columns of
Germans are moving quickly towards the eastern
edge of the town. Gradually, they all disappear; just
swallowed up.

I know where they've gone. It's the crossroads in
our village; the Gheluvelt crossroads. It's hidden
away among ditches and undergrowth, in a steep
little valley. No one will be able to see them. I turn
my head towards the Menin to Zandevoorde Road. I
can see a British division below me. They're looking
as if they might start up towards the village. They
won't know the Germans are waiting for them.
They'll walk into a trap. I must tell them.

I slither down out of my tree faster than a squirrel.
A mist has enveloped us. Good. All the better for me
to try and get to the British forces and warn them.

I'm running, sliding, slipping along the muddy track; falling into potholes and ditches, heading for the road.

'Halt, halt! *Wo gehst du?*'

I look over my shoulder and see a German soldier – all bedraggled and bloodstained. He's pointing a gun at me. I stop. I feel faint and choked with fear. Who'll look after Els if I die?

'Halt!'

His voice is shaky and high like Uncle Henrik's had been when he told us we must leave. 'Halt!' Yet he hardly seems much older than me. His rifle waves around as if he were drunk, so I start running again, half expecting a bullet between my shoulders. I glance over my shoulder. The German has sunk to his knees with his head in his hands. He's weeping.

I get to the road, and over to the other side. I must tell the British. I trip, and find myself tangled in barbed wire. The shells are flying like rain; the rifles hammer out their bullets, and all around I hear moaning and groaning and tearful cries of injured and dying soldiers. Some cry like Els in the night: 'Mummy! I want Mummy. Others moan, *'Mutti!'* *'Maman!'*

I'm on my stomach now. I feel like some primeval creature; a lungfish perhaps, neither fish nor fowl, nor human, as though I had emerged out of some evolutionary swamp, crawling my way across the land, gasping, heaving. More coils of barbed wire; I wriggle round them, over them, through torn gaps where barbs reach out and rip my legs. I teeter on the edge of a trench and look down…

* * *

Don't go, my friend,
  Don't go.
  Allahu – Akbar…
I mumble my dawn prayers. It comforts me to face east; to face Mecca and beyond Mecca to India. As I raise my head from the ground, I see a face peering down at me. Quick as a flash I raise my bayonet. The face vanishes at the same moment as I realise it's only a child. Boy? Girl? I couldn't tell.

'Hey, Mohammed! Wake up. I saw a child; golden-haired; like an angel.'

'Aaah! Go back to sleep,' mutters Mohammed.

* * *

I roll back, shocked. What kind of man was that? If it is a man; brown as the earth; surely not a soldier; a magician perhaps, or an actor; a wandering player;

something out of the Arabian Nights. Instead of a cap on his head, he has a dark green turban; silver buttons gleam like stars on his green jacket, and he's wearing red trousers. Els was right. She had seen a man in red trousers.

Still on my stomach, I wriggle away. At least he's not a German. But where are the British? Then suddenly, a hand grips my collar and hauls me to my feet. 'What the dickens? Where did this piece of… come from?' And a face – another face – a white face – exhausted, covered in mud and grime peers into mine, and I see his peaked cap, and his khaki uniform and boots, and I mutter, 'Tommy? Are you Tommy? English Tommy?'

A shell flies over our heads. He grabs me and we both tumble down into a trench.

'Wanna get killed?' he chokes, wiping the spray of mud from his eyes and nose, while I crouch on my knees doing the same with the end of my smock.

'*Deutscher. Allemands!*' I point frantically towards my village.

Suddenly he gets the message. 'Germans? In Gheluvelt? Better get you to my commanding officer,' he mutters.

* * *

THE MAN IN THE RED TROUSERS

DAWN: 30th October 1914

At six o'clock the bombardment started.

By 08:00 German artillery has destroyed the positions of the 2nd Welch Regiment and the 1st South Wales Borderers Battalion, the 1st Queen's Regiment and two companies of the 2nd King's Royal Rifles are separated from the Welch. The Germans penetrate the gap, killing and wounding 514 ranks with only 16 officers remaining. C.B. Morland, the Commanding Officer of the Welch is killed in action.

Six machine-gunners from the Duke of Connaught's 129th Own Baluchis Regiment are ordered to hold the ridge at Gheluvelt.

There are six of us up on a ridge in Gheluvelt, manning three machine guns. We've been ordered to hold this ridge come what may, to give the rest of them an advantage – something which was not lost on the enemy. The sky is full of balloons. We would think them beautiful, but they are deadly as they float over us, drifting in and out of veils of mist and rain, firing into the British ranks. They've spotted us. With the enemy above and below, the British with their rifles rattling like hailstones, we start shifting our machine guns to higher ground. At the highest point there is one tree standing. We go beneath it, as if somehow it could protect us, even though it is stripped bare with autumn and shrapnel. A small red spotted handkerchief waves limply in the windy rain. We can see them down below, hurling grenades, charging at each other with bayonets fixed. We load, aim fire; load aim, fire; load, aim, fire... We must not give up Gheluvelt.

Load...aim...fire...load...aim...fire.

* * *

I get back after delivering my message, but find the house burning. I scream and scream, 'Els, Els!' I try to find a way in. The heat drives me back. Flames burst from every window. 'Els, Els!' I run round in circles calling her name incessantly till, miraculously, she appears – standing in the doorway of the barn, looking incredibly small, holding Michael's hand. I fall at their feet, crying uncontrollably. The shells are flying all around. One hits the barn. Now that is on fire. I see soldiers pouring into the yard. I can't tell if they are friend or foe. I grab Els and drag her along as I race for my secret tree. Somehow, I can't think of anywhere else to go. Michael follows, swift, but silent as a shadow.

* * *

11.30 am: Gheluvelt is a shambles. The British pour in more support.

13:30 am: No 1 Corps hold a line just 2,000 yards east of Ypres. It has to be held at all costs, or risk the northern flank of Ypres collapsing. 2nd division appear to be holding its own, but at Gheluvelt the situation is serious.

14:30: 2nd Battalion Royal Worcesters arrive at Gheluvelt, and in a rapid counter-attack retake the town.

My name is Khudadad Khan. Will you tell them back home? I did my best. We all did, but I'm the only one left alive. We never left our post or abandoned our machine guns, but kept firing, till one by one, the others dropped dead. Mohammed too. I'm leaning up against this tree. He is cradled in my arms. I held him like that, singing to him, till the light went out of his eyes:

'Don't go, don't go.
Stay back, my friend.'

I rock him now, even though his body is cold, and his spirit has gone.

Then I notice three children standing a little way off, watching me. One of them is the angel.

On 31st October, Khudadad Khan was sent with two companies of the Baluchis to a ridge in the village of Gheluvelt in the Hollebeke Sector. Although greatly outnumbered they fought the enemy all through the day with conspicuous bravery, but were finally overrun by the Germans. All five other men in his detachment were killed with bullets or bayoneted, and their guns smashed, but Khudadad Khan continued working his gun until he himself was badly wounded and left for dead. Despite his wounds, he waited till nightfall before he managed to crawl back to his regiment. Thanks to the bravery of Khudadad Khan and his fellow Baluchis, they managed to keep the Germans at bay long enough for reinforcements to arrive. They strengthened the line and thus prevented the Germans from reaching the vital ports along the Belgian and French coastline.

* * *

The man in the red trousers stopped singing when he saw us, and became so still, I wondered if he too had died. We had shuffled close together, holding hands, and just stood there, I don't know how long. Then he turned and looked at us and, in that look, I saw despair, grief, bewilderment and wonder.

It was Michael who ran forward and offered him a turnip.

'Oh, and he must be thirsty too,' I cried. And I rushed off to fetch some water. It took me ages to find a cup, fill it from the stream and come back. By the time I returned Michael and Els were sitting on the ground next to the strange soldier. Night was falling, and the drizzle which had barely stopped all day was turning to fine snow. I gave him the cup, and he looked up at me with eyes which brimmed with all the sorrows of the world, then he pulled one of the silver buttons off his jacket and gave it to me.

We had all fallen asleep huddled together under my tree as the rain turned to snow sprinkling over the scene, so that anyone passing may not have known which were the corpses and which the sleepers.

It was almost dawn when I awoke. We were covered with a green army jacket. Els was pressed into my back, but where was Michael – and where was the man in the red trousers? They had both gone.

He must have told them about us, as some Tommies came by and put us in a truck which took us to the coast. I asked them about Michael. 'Where is he?'

But they looked vague. 'A Baluchi soldier did

make it through the night back to his regiment, and someone saw a boy helping him. But no one knows who he was or where he went.'

My name is Lotte Becke. My sister is called Els. We were put on a boat to England and looked after by a very nice English family. We're not sure why we're alive when so many died. I wish I knew what happened to Michael.

At the end of the war, my father found us and took us home.

I keep the silver button with me wherever I go. It reminds me of the man in the red trousers, and I think it brings me luck.

For his matchless feat of courage and gallantry,
Sepoy Khudadad Khan was awarded the
Victoria Cross.

PROPPING UP THE LINE
Ian Beck

Author's note:

'Propping up the Line' is partly based on the experiences of my maternal grandfather, Alfred Gauntlett. He was gassed in the First World War – he survived the attack, but eventually died in early middle age. His lungs were so badly damaged that he could only work in the summer. He said very little to any of his family about his experiences in France. When the call came to write something about the First World War, I realised that I had a chance to write about Alfred and, mostly through invention, I have done my best to honour his story and his sacrifice.

Alfred felt something move. It came out of the mud in the dark behind his back where he sat cold and drowsily slumped against the trench wall. Something small and warmly alive pushed itself between the wooden slats and his battledress jacket. It touched for an instant the small exposed area of his pale dirty skin just where his jacket and vest were folded and rucked up together. He could feel something struggling and pushing to get past him. He shot up in revulsion – he knew just what it was: a filthy—

'*Rat!*' he shouted to no one in particular.

He saw it there, pushing through and twisting its head, saw the wet greasy fur and its mean red eyes. He kicked at it and missed. The rat scuttled out from the tiny gap between the slat supports and ran across the mud. Normally Alfred would have let it go. Rats were, after all, commonplace but something, whether pent-up anger…hate…loss…pain…boredom, whichever it was made him give chase after it.

The creature appeared sluggish, as if it were weighed down with overeating. It had most likely been feeding on what was caught, left behind, in the lines and coils of barbed wire which stretched for miles beyond the trench. The terrible sad detritus of dead soldiers. The remains that were left behind after a 6am push.

Before it was light, after the heavy artillery bombardments and the whistles and the bright spray of the flares and the shouting and the Very lights, the men streamed over, filtered through the narrow gaps in the wire. Whole portions of them however were miraculously left behind like tea leaves caught in a strainer – bits of men hooked up and hanging there for all to see, like the display in an awful butcher's shop window; or if there were enough shreds and rags of uniform still attached to the lumps and limbs, then it was more like the washing on the line flapping on a Monday morning at home.

Alfred had grown almost used to such sights.

Almost used to the red-raw and random collops being the remains of men he had sometimes known and shared fag time and mugs of tea with.

Almost used to them being suddenly torn apart and scattered around here and there or falling like rain into the mud.

Almost used to them being thrown up like jacks in the air along with the astonishingly loud shellbursts.

Used to seeing the severed remains chucked around among the living like so much discarded offal. Used to seeing legs, hands, halves of heads, and sometimes neatly sliced and sheared-off faces stare up at him blankly from the grey mud. Used to seeing his pals' slippery insides suddenly all spilled out from between their buttons, or poking through the rips and gaps in their khakis. Used to seeing their innards hanging like obscene posthumous medals across their tunics. Wet yellow, grey and red, and fully exposed in the cold light of the outside where they didn't belong at all. Where they were never meant to be seen. He knew it was wrong to be even remotely used to such sights, or to any of it, even for a second, let alone for ever...

The rat zigzagged through the mud down the service trench, past the wooden sign to Piccadilly Circus. It hesitated at the base of a trench ladder, and Alfred finally smashed it down into the mud. He felt its tiny backbone crack under his boot and he had a moment of fleeting sympathy for it: just another dirty dead thing, another of God's creatures that had given up the ghost in the mud like so many others, and no one there to grieve its loss but him. He twisted his boot on the rat, pushing its bloated little body further into the mire.

Private Jones was sitting there in the gloom among the sandbags, throwing a cricket ball up in the air and catching it again.

'Fancy a game, Alfred?' he said with a grin.

'Bit dark, Jonesey, ain't it, bit bloody cold too,' Alfred said, rubbing his hands together. He had shaped up a cricket bat of sorts using a bayonet as a spoke shave, and sometimes they played a bit as best they could, up the line near the blasted little wood not far from the dressing station under the nets.

'Look lively, Alfred, Jonesey, job for you two,' Sergeant Trewin said as he emerged from the dark bunker. He was a weary thick-set Cornishman, short-limbed and with heavy black stubble all round his fierce chops. He held a pair of wire cutters out in his hand. 'Up and over and widen the gaps in the wire, lads, big push tomorrow. Alfred, you and Jonesey step to now and keep your heads down. Gas helmets at the ready – they do like to send 'em over in the dark.'

Private Jones, Jonesey, was younger than Alfred, no more than eighteen and clumsy with it. He was keen on cricket and surprisingly good with the bat. He had shorn-off bright ginger stubble at his neck and his blue-white skin was all covered over with freckles. Alfred didn't give him long at best.

But gaps were needed in the protective barbed wire. If the wire wasn't opened up before a push, then it caused a bottleneck and that meant more 'leaves in the strainer' and more 'washing on the line'.

Two cutters to go out in the dark beyond the trench: one to hold, one to cut. This was tough work. Alfred thanked God for his thick leather gloves. There had been a sniper a day or so before high up on the ridge, he knew, but the Jerry seemed to have fallen silent. Perhaps he had been killed or just gone away; who knew?

They climbed the ladder out of the relative safety of the trench and crouched down close to the cold mud, then they ran one behind the other across the few yards of dead earth to the wire. Jonesey had no gloves, so he got to cut while Alfred did his best to pull the strands of sharp cold wire apart inch by inch, slow work.

There was a wood behind them half a mile or so up the incline and Alfred heard an owl screech from somewhere among what was left of the trees. He was amazed that anything was left alive among those blasted and denuded stumps. It had been the same a few short months ago when he had heard and seen larks rising and singing above the fields during a bombardment

Jonesey was crouching next to him at mud level when Alfred heard a familiar brisk firework sound like 'crack'.

'Gas,' he shouted at once, in a shivering panic. He fumbled for his respirator. A gas bomb gone off, and close.

Jonesey was all fingers and thumbs. He had the wire cutters in his hand and he hesitated, not wanting to drop them in the mud and lose them. The sickly sweet smell drifted low. There was a gong clash from the trench – the alarm – and Sergeant Trewin also shouting, 'Gas…'

There were twenty to thirty seconds at most in which to get the mask on. Alfred had his more or less fixed when he saw through the smeared lenses that Jonesey was still fumbling at his waist, poking about with his free hand, the cutters still in the other.

'Chrissakes,' Alfred said, wrenching at Jonesey's mask and trying to pull it up for him.

The gas billowed in then, palpable and thick. Jonesey, unbalanced and still crouched down as if to cut, fell onto his back in the mud. He floundered there for a moment like an upended turtle, his mask pressed under him in the gloop…and he breathed in the gas.

He eventually drowned in the mud alone. Drowned in the froth of his own blood. The foaming heated discharge of Jonesey's lungs bubbled in his mouth and blistered his lips, which wouldn't open again even to let him scream. First, though, he vomited and rolled over in the mud in agony.

Alfred threw himself down next to him, hardly able to see a thing. The dying boy's arm flailed upwards and knocked Alfred's mask aside for a moment or two and Alfred too breathed in a measure of the gas before he could swing his mask back round.

He abandoned the position. He abandoned the dead Jonesey and rolled and staggered back across the sticky sucking muddy ground and finally fell down into the trench. He lay beneath the ladder, and the only thing he could make out in the dark and the agony was Jonesey's cricket ball...

He coughed and felt the strong stabbing pain in his chest and was suddenly breathless. He gripped the ladder.

'You alright, mate? Steady now,' Sergeant Trewin said from behind his mask.

Alfred said to himself under his breath, 'Steady now...steady,' and passed out.

Alfred's little daughter Nell first heard the news from a telegram. A telegraph boy knocked on the door one morning. He was very smart in his uniform and little Nell, Alfred's youngest, only four years old, could see part of his bright red bicycle propped up against the front garden wall. Alice, her mother, didn't want to open the telegram there and then, so she waited until the boy had cycled off. She closed the front door and then stood in the hall with her back to the door, holding up the envelope.

Olive, Nell's older sister said, 'What is it, Mum?'

'A telegram, dear,' Alice said, her voice trembling, almost breaking. She went through into the kitchen and sat at the table with the envelope still unopened in her hand. The canary was singing. The sunlight slanted in on her cage which hung in the window.

Nell stood by the table, her eyes level with the top while Alice opened the envelope and carefully unfolded the telegram, not liking to look at it too closely.

'It's Alfred,' she said. 'Dad...Dad's been gassed,' she added, and then quietly after a moment and with a catch in her voice, 'He's still alive...still.'

The gas had burned into his lungs. The mustard gas. They said men drowned of the gas. And they did; they were burned on the outside, their skin blistering and leaching yellow pus. Inside, their lungs filled with liquid and froth and blood, and then they drowned in their own fluids, like poor Jonesey.

Burned and drowned.

Alfred had survived.

* * *

It was her mother's hand that Nell concentrated on during the walk to the seafront. She couldn't think about her dad properly. It was exciting that he was finally coming home, but it was also frightening.

She hardly knew him, hadn't seen him for so long that she couldn't remember what he really looked like at all. She remembered his smell, though, or thought she did: tobacco and fresh sawdust. She felt badly about it, as if she had somehow shut him out or given up on him, but she didn't dare tell anyone that, not even her big sister Olive. She clutched her mother's kind fingers in their summer-weight cotton gloves, as she was pulled along behind her. She felt the squeezing comfort, the presence of the reassuring hand. She could feel the nub of the hard little covered button at her mother's wrist too, and she played with the shape of it as they drew nearer to the seafront.

Her mother stopped for a moment, looked down at Nell and smiled, and her eyes looked suddenly big behind her glasses. 'Be good now, Nellie dear,' she said, 'and be brave for Dad.'

Olive held onto Nell's other hand. They heard the sound of a silver band which drifted from the seafront.

* * *

Alfred waited for his family on the seafront in the glitter of the unlikely sunshine. It seemed almost too bright and too clean. The Salvation Army band struck up 'Eternal Father, Strong to Save', and he turned and looked seaward. He watched the breakers crashing onto the pebbles and breathed the brisk bright salt air into his ruined lungs with a gasp.

He had thought he would never see any of the old country or any of his little family again, yet now here he was, in the middle of it all, and it was like a bank holiday: bright sunlight, scudding clouds, flags, bunting and a fresh wind on the seafront promenade – just as he had often imagined over in the field hospital in that other place. Here he was with a dozen or so others – others, who, for all he knew, might be a lot worse off than himself. Certainly one of them had half of one leg gone, his uniform trouser leg safety-pinned up and flapping empty below the knee.

Then he saw them through the crowd. They had crossed the road and were coming towards him over the lawns – Alice and the two girls, his two precious girls: Olive and Ellen, little Nellie. They were all turned out in their Sunday best, white dresses and white ribbons in their hair, and Alice in a hat. He broke ranks, stepped forward just once, his arm raised in a wave.

Olive, his eldest daughter, ran to him and threw her arms tight round his waist, and her hair smelled clean like the bright sea air. Alice and Nell stood back a way, Nell holding onto her mother's hand.

'I doubt Nell even remembers me,' Alfred said as he walked over to them, tugging an excited and tearful Olive along by the hand.

Their mother was, as ever, dignified – remote, even. She held onto her hat tight to her head with one hand in the brisk wind.

Alfred nodded to her and said matter of factly, 'A good drying day,' and then, 'Who's this little girl, then, who's all grown up, let me look?'

Nell stared up at him her eyes narrowed.

'Ask me the time, then,' he said, looking down at her.

'What's the time?' she said, a smile spreading across her face as she remembered something. A game, a tease they had; and she was suddenly remembering more now, knowing just what was to come.

He pretended to take out a fob watch. Made as if to click the lid open. 'Why,' he said, 'it's half past chisel, a quarter to sandpaper,' and delighted in her giggling response. The happy sound of unforced laughter; he hadn't heard *that* for a while.

His wife Alice, still clutching onto her hat, finally

leaned in to her husband and kissed his cheek. 'Welcome home, Alfred,' she said.

When they arrived back at the house Alfred saw that there was a group of neighbours out to meet him. Mr Shearing was out from number five in his waistcoat and he shook Alfred's hand. 'Good to have you back, Alfred, how are you?' he said, and gave him a pat on the shoulder.

Olive finally let go of her father's hand and said, pointing up to the space above their front door, 'I put that flag up there.'

Nell said, 'And I helped. I held onto the chair carefully so she didn't fall down.'

'I'm sure you both did very well,' Alfred said, looking up at the Union flag stretched out behind the glass panel. 'Time to take it down now, though, I think, girls.'

He was tired suddenly; fed up with the bright glare of the sun, the fast blustery white clouds, the smiling neighbours, the sense of being brightly lit on a stage and being gawked at. He knew they were there to look him over for signs, for clues as to what it might have been like away in that other country, and here he was the traveller returned. But he couldn't tell them anything, not now or ever. He just wanted indoors, calm and a cup of tea.

PROPPING UP THE LINE

* * *

He sat in his old place at the kitchen table, a table he had made with his own hands. The brown teapot sat under its knitted cosy while the tea brewed. Home-made cake sat on a plate and the canary chirped in her cage in the scullery window. Olive had been sent off to play quietly with Nell upstairs.

Alfred was alone with Alice. She sat looking over at him, her hand extended across the smooth surface of the table and she was just able to touch his short square-ended fingers. He did not hold her hand yet, all of that would come in time.

There were so many things he could say and perhaps should say. He should tell Alice everything that had happened – but he couldn't bring himself to mention any of it. Not to Alice, and not to anyone else either. Even though he should be able to share anything and everything with her, he knew that he couldn't share that nightmare of chaos. Nothing at all, in fact, of what had happened there, not one jot or tickle of it could ever be shared. Even if he were to share it, in any case he knew that he would not be believed. No, it was a burden best kept locked away safely inside his head in the dark, saved up for bad dreams. Kept cold like the joint of a half leg of lamb in the meat safe, or like poor Jonesey in the mud.

He drank his welcome tea, ate his cake – Alice

was as skilled as a baker as he was as a carpenter. Both had capable 'making' hands.

'Nell's grown so much,' he said finally.

The next morning Nell was sent to buy a loaf all on her own from Mr Dummer's shop round the corner in Stoneham Road. The coins to pay for the loaf, wrapped in a twist of blue sugar paper, the exact money, were held very tightly in her hot hand all the way. It was the first time she had been sent to buy anything on her own.

Alice had sent her so that she could wash through the shamed and bloodstained pillowcase from the bed while Olive waited for Nell out on the doorstep.

Mrs Dummer unwrapped the pennies, counted them and then gave Nell the loaf, loosely swathed in a sheet of white paper. 'Don't want flour all on your nice dress, do we now?' she said, wiping the sweat from her forehead with her sleeve.

Back home, Alfred put a slice of the fresh bread on the tines of the toasting fork. He held it out to the fire and soon the bread was scorched and the edges and crust were browned and then almost blackened.

'That's how we made our toast,' he said quietly, and then his head jerked round suddenly to face Nell and his eyes were wet and rimmed raw-red. 'Sodding blasted Army rations,' he said, allowing the curtain to part slightly and his voice to be suddenly edgy and harsh.

To Nell, it felt like a stone thrown towards her. Her dad looked down at the crisp edges of the toasted bread as Nell, frightened, backed away from him and from his staring eyes and went quietly out to the kitchen without a word.

Every evening now, their mother took a white china basin from the larder and part-filled it with hot water and Friar's Balsam. Alfred sat at the table and the girls watched as he breathed as best he could through the pungent fumes. His head and the basin were covered over and bound together by the draped towel, just as when the canary needed to be silenced.

Alice held his hand and spoke quietly to him. 'That's it, Alfred, breathe it in now, it'll do you good.'

The whole kitchen smelled of the balsam and the fumes caught at the back of Alfred's throat and he coughed. The cough was harsh and wet, but muffled a little by the towel. And the more he coughed, the further Nell hid behind Olive or her mother, sometimes going back as far as the dark larder.

* * *

Alfred's toolbox had waited for him. Solid square and patient, it had sat there through all the months that he had been away, the tools still bright and sharp in their neat rows. It was one of the proofs that his former life really had existed. It had all seemed so remote, so far away and so finished and done with over there in that other place, as if his other life had died with him the moment he had crossed the sea. He had never thought he would see his toolbox or smell fresh-cut sawdust again. It was all there, though, ready and only too willing – like a dog keen for the lead – to be buckled onto the shoulder strap and used again.

He set off to work one cold morning. They were building streets of new houses and he had been hired to help make the staircases. There was a big corrugated shed on the building site where the larger-scale carpentry was set to be carried out. It was fitted out with benches and lathes.

Alfred wore his soft hat and muffler and the box of tools were on the strap over his shoulder. But even the short walk from the house winded him. He had to stop to catch his breath, holding onto a lamppost before he had even crossed Portland Road.

The sides of the carpentry shed were open to the weather and the cold air bit through him and made him wheezy. It was no good – he had to go home and rest.

Clearly he couldn't work outside, or at all in the winter.

Every Monday morning there was always a big tin bath full of wet washing. Monday was washing day all up the street. Mrs Bedford next door pegged out washing in her garden on one side, and Mrs Lack in her garden on the other side. Nell helped Alice with the wash and Mrs Lack usually talked to Nell over the wall.

If it was cloudy or had been raining she would smile and point to a patch of blue in the sky and say, 'See there, Nelly, soon be enough blue to make a sailor's suit.'

Nell always tried to see the sailor in the patches of blue sky, but somehow she muddled it all up in her mind with poor Mr Lack who had been a sailor and who had drowned in the sea.

Alfred watched and waited from the kitchen as they put the washing through the mangle. Nell held up one side while Alice turned the handle and pulled each of the things through between the wooden rollers. He could hear the squeezed-out water splash down hard onto the area paving below the window – it sounded like Jonesey's vomit splattering onto the mud after the gas bomb.

When they had finished and pegged everything to the line, Alice called out, 'Alfred.'

Here was his job; here was something he could do. He picked up the long wooden clothes prop and pushed the forked end up tight against the washing line. Then he lifted all the heavy wet washing up into the bright windy air.

He secured the prop by pushing it down hard into the short grass and looked up at all the shirts and shifts, the pillowcases and socks, the bloomers and the sheets. They flapped overhead in the wind all across the back gardens, the clothes fluttering like flags, like the fragments of men and uniform caught up on the wire. The washing was an army of occupation, with their line going as far as the little lilac tree by the wall.

Alfred closed his eyes and listened to the flap and crack of the cloth in the wind. He tried to catch his breath as the shadows moved back and forth across the grass.

Nell looked to where he was standing. His upper half was just a rippling blue shadow cast across the white sheets. The shadow stood there, its head bowed, its mouth wide trying to breathe, both hands still held tight to the tall wooden prop.

* * *

One morning the rag and bone man and his cart clopped up the street. Alfred watched the rag man's cart as it passed further up the road with the slow tread of hooves. The load of junk was roughly covered over with a dun-coloured tarpaulin. Alice and Nell were in the doorway just behind Alfred, and some impulse made him point over at the cart with the stem of his unlit pipe and say to them, 'See that, there's a million dead boys piled up under there on that cart, a million of them or more.'

Nell stepped back and allowed herself to be safely hidden – but still fearful – in the folds of her mother's apron.

'What a thing to say in front of poor Nellie, Alfred,' Alice said.

One morning Nell was out in the garden, sitting on a tree stump, all burrowed under the fuchsia bush and watching the bees as they went in and out of the flowers. Bugles and drums started up very loudly nearby. The Boy's Brigade band were practising in the Stoneham Road Baptist Church Hall.

Alfred came out of the back door and stood near to where Nell was hidden – he didn't notice her sitting down there so very quiet and close in the shadow of the big fuchsia all buzzing with the bees.

He looked towards the open back windows of the church hall and he listened to the drums and the bugles and the marching tunes. The band played 'Onward Christian Soldiers' and he started coughing and couldn't stop. His head slumped forward onto his chest and he reached his arms up and held onto the tight washing line just above his head. He almost swung there for a moment, caught on the line, his arms wide, coughing while his toecaps slipped across the grass.

Nell stood up, frightened and unsure of what to do. While the bugles still called across the gardens, she moved out of the shade and went and stood next to her father and Alfred looked down at her, his face red from coughing. One of his arms hung over the washing line at the crook of the elbow. Nell had her doll's handkerchief tucked in her sleeve, so she pulled it out and offered it to him. She stood on tiptoe and Alfred reached down and took the little hankie from her, then wiped his mouth on it, even though the hankie was small and of real use only to a doll. There were spots of blood on the hankie when he had finished.

'Didn't see you there,' he said. 'See, I'm coughing even in the warm weather now, but sshhh, don't say anything to Mum.'

* * *

PROPPING UP THE LINE

They went out one Sunday to watch a cricket match. They sat in deckchairs, down from the pavilion near the boundary rope. Olive plaited Nellie's hair while they watched and later on in the afternoon, after the tea interval, as the shadows lengthened across the grass, Alice took Olive over to the Ladies.

One of the young batsmen squeezed his way out between the row of deckchairs and Alfred stood up to make way for him. The young man had cropped bright ginger hair and his cricket bat was sloped onto his shoulder like a rifle. As he walked out just beyond the boundary rope, Alfred called after him, 'I should have done more for you, Jonesey.' And then, 'I could have done more. If only you hadn't been on your back like that.'

The player turned briefly and looked back at Alfred, nodded and then made his way to the crease. He took up his position and measured out a dummy defensive stroke with a straight bat. All the players on the field were transformed suddenly by the late sunlight appearing from behind a cloud. The light flooded across the green, casting long shadows and a nimbus of light around their heads.

Nell had been sitting at her father's feet. She looked up at him, puzzled by what he had said. He was still standing lost in thought, shielding his eyes from the low sun...

* * *

The last of the family now, at the age of ninety-six, Nell – her mind drifting between then and now and everything muddled between past and present – for no real reason was sorting through a messy sideboard drawer. Tucked away at the back behind a tightly folded envelope she found her father's pipe.

It was cold to the touch, and when she took it out and held it she felt suddenly four years old again. She could see Alfred clearly, pointing, jabbing with the pipe stem towards the covered rag and bone cart as it passed by outside their old house.

Close to death now herself, she remembered what he had said. He had been through so much, seen so much and he never had said anything much to anyone – just that once…

The folded paper inside the envelope was his death certificate, signed by poor Olive who had to go and register it. *Alfred Gauntlett, Carpenter, died of congested heart failure brought on by complications with bronchitis and asthma.*

Nell pointed with the pipe at the windows of her flat, and as the sunlight slanted in suddenly she heard a canary singing.

'What's the time, Dad?' she said, smiling in anticipation of the teasing answer which never came.

WHAT'S IN A NAME
Nigel Hinton

Author's note:

My grandfather was Polish. His family was very poor and there wasn't enough to eat, so at the age of ten he left his home and walked two hundred miles to the sea. He got a job as a cabin boy on a boat and went round the world a couple of times. When he was fourteen, he landed in London and stayed. His surname was Hinz. To show his loyalty to his new country when the First World War started, he changed it to Hinton. This story is in honour of him.

All the terrible things started after the Zeppelin raids.

At the beginning of the war, a lot of people turned against anything that sounded German and some boys at school made a few nasty remarks about Wilhelm's name. He'd even been called 'a dirty Hun'. It had hurt, of course, but he'd pretended he didn't care and after a while the teasing and hostility stopped.

But everything changed when the Zeppelin bombing raids started. The fear seemed to send people mad.

Even before the raids actually began, all kinds of wild rumours swept round: some people said that bombs were going to fall every night, others said that there would be gas attacks and some even said that poisoned food would be dropped from the airships. The whole city seemed to be waiting for something terrible to happen and Wilhelm was as nervous as everyone else.

The first two raids on London were far away across the other side of the Thames. There were pictures of the damage and lists of the casualties in all the newspapers, but Wilhelm still couldn't imagine what it would actually be like to have death and destruction raining down from the sky. On the night of 7th September 1915 he found out.

He was jolted out of sleep by the sound of a distant explosion. A moment later there was another one – it sounded closer. Then another – definitely closer. There was a bright flash outside the window and the whole house shook. He jumped out of bed and raced down the stairs. Papa was standing on the front doorstep. Mama was holding onto Papa's arm and trying to pull him back inside the house. Down the hill, towards the River Thames, flames were shooting into the sky. There were two more explosions and Mama cried out and covered her ears. Wilhelm went and stood next to Papa at the front door. People were running up the hill, screaming and shouting.

One of the running men, pointed and shouted, 'There it is.' The clouds parted briefly and very high up in the sky was a cigar-shaped airship glowing silvery gold in the light of the moon. It was moving away from Greenwich and heading towards Deptford. Shortly afterwards there were more explosions but a few minutes later they stopped and there was just the orange glow from the fires reflected in the misty sky.

The next morning there was a smell of smoke in the air and on his way to school Wilhelm passed a house that had been hit by an incendiary bomb. It was still smouldering and firemen were pumping water onto it. People were standing in the street, staring at the wrecked building as if they couldn't believe what had happened and Wilhelm knew how they felt. War was no longer far away in France or in Turkey where his brother, Kristof, was fighting. It was here. Here, near his home. Perhaps his house would be the next to be hit.

When he got to school everyone was talking about the raid and Bill Richardson was showing the cut on his hand that he'd got from flying glass when a bomb exploded down his street and broke the windows in his house.

'Why are they dropping bombs on civilians?' Bill said. 'It isn't war – it's murder.'

'What do you expect?' Edwin Lambert said. 'The Germans aren't human beings like us. They're monsters, worse than beasts!'

Everyone nodded. Nobody ever disagreed with Edwin. He was big and strong and he had a quick temper and even quicker fists. Sometimes Wilhelm longed to contradict some of the stupid things he said, but he never had the nerve.

'I heard there were over twenty people killed,' Tom Grant said.

'Twenty last night. How many next?' Edwin

Lambert said, then he looked directly at Wilhelm when he added, 'My father reckons there were probably German spies on the ground showing the Zeppelin the way to go with signals from torches.'

Luckily, no one else followed that idea up and the moment passed, but all day Wilhelm felt as if people were giving him strange looks and hardly anyone spoke to him. He tried to tell himself that he was imagining it all but he couldn't help feeling lonely, especially when he couldn't find Harry Clark at the end of school. They were best friends and they always walked home together. Was Harry avoiding him too?

There was another raid the next night. The bombs dropped further upriver near Rotherhithe but the explosions jerked Wilhelm out of sleep again and he lay awake for the rest of the night waiting for a bomb to fall. Would you hear it coming or would you just be blown to smithereens in an instant?

Edwin Lambert and a couple of his older friends were leaning against the wall when Wilhelm walked into the playground in the morning.

'Your bloody lot were at it again last night,' Lambert called.

Wilhelm knew he should ignore it but he couldn't.

'What do you mean – my lot? I was born here. I'm as British as you are.'

'British? With a father called Heinrich Linz? What kind of Hun name is that? He's a butcher, isn't he?'

'Yes – so what?'

'Well, I wouldn't eat meat from his shop – it's probably poisoned. They ought to put him in that internment camp at Alexandra Palace with all the other aliens.'

'We're not aliens. We're British.'

Lambert spat on the ground in front of Wilhelm, then turned away and started talking to his friends. Wilhelm walked into the school but he was shaking with anger and...what was it? Fear? Yes, he felt scared. Terrible times were coming – he just knew it.

That night he was woken up by the sound of breaking glass but it wasn't caused by bombs. When he ran downstairs Mama was standing in the open doorway. She was crying. Papa was out in the street, staring at the broken window of his shop.

'Vhy they throw bricks? Vhat they vant I do?' Papa said, and Wilhelm was aware of how strong his accent sounded. 'I have British passport, no? My first son he join the British army. I love this country, no? And they do this.'

His hand was trembling as he pointed to the wall next to the front door. There, in big white letters, was the word: HUN.

The next day the shop window was replaced and Papa hung a big Union Jack behind it. That didn't stop the vandals. The window was smashed again during the night.

Papa replaced the window. And it was broken again.

This time he nailed boards over the window. Someone painted the words HUN and SPY on the boards. Mama spent hours scrubbing the board, but the ghostly shape of the letters could still be seen. Papa took the Union Jack and nailed it across the boards. No one touched the flag, but four days later they were all sitting in the living room above the shop when someone threw a stone through the window.

Flying glass cut Mama's face and she sobbed in terror for hours in case the vandals came back. 'Maybe they burn us. I have heard they make fires of houses.'

They didn't come back. A month went by.

Papa took the boards down and replaced the window. He hung the Union Jack in the window but often, when Wilhelm got home from school, the shop was empty. Trade was bad. Papa was hopeful at first – his meat was the best in the area, people would soon come back and buy it again.

But weeks passed and still customers shunned the shop. Papa grew more and more gloomy and silent.

At the same time, Kristof's letters stopped coming and Mama became convinced that something terrible had happened to him. Wilhelm began to think that things couldn't get worse. But they did. Tom Grant's older brother was killed in the fighting near the French town of Artois.

The headmaster announced the news at morning assembly and there was a stunned silence in the hall. It wasn't the first time that an old boy from the school had been killed but John Grant was different. He had been head boy only two years before and everybody still remembered him. He had been a sort of hero to the whole school – a top sportsman, a brilliant student, always smiling and kind. And now he was dead.

Tom Grant was away from school for a week. Wilhelm tried to imagine what he was feeling. What would it be like if Kristof was killed?

A hush fell over everyone when Tom finally walked back into the classroom one morning. He looked pale and his eyes had dark rings under them. He went to his desk and sat down. Nobody moved. Frozen – not knowing what to do or say. The silence went on for nearly a minute, then Wilhelm went over. He would say what no one else could.

'We're all awfully sorry to hear about John. He was a top chap.'

Tom raised his eyes. They were full of tears. Then he stood up and the tears ran down his face.

'You Germans killed him,' Tom said. There was no anger in his voice, just a terrible flat coldness.

It was like being punched in the stomach and Wilhelm took a step back. He liked Tom. He was a friend. How could he say something so terrible?

'Steady on, Tom – I'm not German. You know that.'

Tom stared at him then sat down, put his arms on the desk and slumped forward to hide his face.

There was a murmur in the classroom. And Wilhelm heard footsteps. A hand pulled him back and spun him round. It was Edwin Lambert.

'Leave him alone. You heard him – he doesn't want to talk to Huns.'

'I'm not a Hun.' Wilhelm could hear that he sounded like a silly little boy with a trembling voice. But he couldn't help it. The whole thing had blown up so fast. 'I'm British. My father and mother were born Polish, but they're British now. They hate the Germans as much as you do.'

'Linz? That's not Polish. Why have you got a Hun name?' Lambert said and stepped closer.

'Because my family came from Prussia originally.'

'Prussia! That's the same as German.'

'No it's not.' Wilhelm could feel his heart

thumping. The blood pulsing in his neck. He mustn't show he was scared. He mustn't. Lambert would love that.

'You say you're Polish and now it turns out you're Prussian.'

'No! Our ancestors came from Prussia over a hundred years ago but they became Polish.'

'They change all the time, don't they, your kind? Prussian, Polish. And now they are pretending to be British.'

'Leave him alone, Lambert!' It was Harry Clark. He came and stood next to Wilhelm. 'Of course he's British. His brother's in the British Army. What's pretending about that?'

'He's not fighting, is he? Just working in some hospital,' Lambert said.

Having Harry standing next to him, knowing that he was still his friend, gave Wilhelm the courage to stand up for Kristof.

He looked Lambert in the eye and spoke with pride. 'He was training to be a doctor – that's why they wanted him in the Medical Corps to help the wounded.'

'Oh yes, where? Somewhere nice and quiet in Africa.'

'He's at Gallipoli. And that's in Turkey, not Africa.'

'Gallipoli,' Lambert sneered. 'Nobody cares about Gallipoli. They didn't send him to France because they thought he'd probably sneak over and join the German army.'

There was a big laugh from the other boys and Lambert grinned at having scored a point.

'You don't know anything, Lambert. You're just an idiot!'

As soon as Wilhelm said it, he realised he'd made a mistake. He should have stayed calm, not lost his temper.

'Did you call me an idiot?' Lambert's eyes were wide and flecks of spit flew from his mouth.

'I—'

'Right, we'll settle this behind the gym after school tomorrow.'

Those dreaded words – 'behind the gym'. Lambert had called him out. It meant a fight. A fight to settle a score. A fight for honour.

Behind the gym was where disputes were settled. Teachers knew it happened but they never interfered. They thought it was the best way for boys to sort out differences. It was all part of the school tradition.

And the tradition had rules. The two fighters had to have seconds. Each second carried a towel to throw on the ground when their fighter had had enough. But if you wanted other boys to respect you, you never allowed the towel to be thrown even if you were being badly beaten.

'Tomorrow,' Lambert said, and held out his hand. Another tradition – you had to shake hands to agree the fight. Wilhelm hesitated. Lambert was a fierce fighter. But only cowards refused to turn up when they had been called out.

Wilhelm took Lambert's hand and shook it.

'I'll be your second tomorrow, if you want,' Harry said as they walked home after school.

'Thanks, Harry – you're a pal. Are you sure, though? Lambert might turn against you too.'

'I don't care about Lambert.'

'You're the only one. I bet the rest of the class will take his side,' Wilhelm said.

'Only because they're scared of him. Most of them will be secretly hoping you win.'

'No chance of that!'

He took hours to get to sleep that night. His mind raced. He thought of the beating he was going to get. Lambert always won. And his opponents always ended up bleeding and bruised. Could he call it off? Apologise to him? No, he would be branded a coward.

When he awoke in the grey early morning light,

the fears rushed back at him and he lay there feeling sick. Then he remembered the awful things Lambert had said. He'd wanted to put Papa in an internment camp. He'd even sneered at what Kristof was doing. That was the worst insult – Kristof was a hero. He could have stayed at medical school but he'd volunteered to join the army. Wilhelm had read about the fighting at Gallipoli and he knew that it was terrible and bloody. Tens of thousands of men had died there and Kristof had had the courage to face that.

Lambert wasn't fit to kiss Kristof's boots. He was just an ignorant bully. He was the one who ought to say sorry. Perhaps he was one of the vandals who had attacked Papa's shop and painted the slogans on the walls.

A kind of wild anger built up inside Wilhelm. No, he wouldn't apologise to Lambert. He would fight him. He would defend his family's name. He would probably lose in the end but he would go down fighting.

Word about the fight had gone round, and as Wilhelm went into the changing rooms to get ready when school finished he saw a crowd of boys heading towards the back of the gym. His stomach turned over in panic. Lambert was already in the changing room. He was in gym kit, flexing his muscles and talking with his second. For a moment Wilhelm thought again of calling the fight off, but then he remembered Kristof and he stripped and put on his shorts and vest. Harry handed him a pair of boxing gloves.

'No gloves,' Lambert called. 'Bare-knuckle.'

'That's not right! It's always gloves,' Harry protested.

'Bare-knuckle or throw in the towel now,' Lambert's second said.

'Bare-knuckle then,' Wilhelm said.

'Wilhelm, no,' Harry said.

'It's fine.' He smiled and nodded at Harry, but a shiver ran up his back.

They walked out of the door and round the side of the building to where the crowd was waiting. The boys had formed a square and left a narrow passage for the fighters and the seconds to walk into the centre.

'Come on, Britain,' someone called, and Wilhelm realised that people were trying to make the fight like a war. Britain against Germany.

Quick as a flash, Wilhelm turned to the boy who had called out, bowed and said, 'Thank you – I'll do my best to represent Britain bravely. Steady the Buffs!'

Some boys laughed and a couple of others clapped

and someone at the back of the crowd shouted, 'Come on, Wilhelm.'

'Come on, Edwin,' some of Lambert's friends called.

The seconds stepped into opposite corners of the square.

The chilly December wind blew and Wilhelm shivered.

'Ready?' Lambert's second said.

'Ready,' Harry said.

'Fight! Fight!' the crowd shouted in unison.

Wilhelm raised his fists and moved forward. Lambert stood his ground and Wilhelm prepared to land the first punch. He pulled his arm back to swing but Lambert suddenly darted back and skipped to the side. As Wilhelm turned towards him, Lambert punched him in the guts, knocking the wind out of him, then followed up with a crunching blow to the face.

Wilhelm's head jerked backwards with an explosion of light. Tears flooded his eyes and when he ran his hand across the bottom of his nose it came away covered in blood. Before he could get his defence up, Lambert hit him again on the side of the head then again on his jaw. He felt his knees buckle and he fell to the ground.

His ears were ringing and the excited shouts from

the crowd seemed far away. He crawled onto all fours and saw blood dripping onto the ground in front of him. Feet were shuffling near him – a pair of plimsolls. They must belong to Lambert. They were moving backwards and forwards as if he was dancing. Behind them were dozens of shoes. He peered up through blurred eyes at the faces staring down at him. He saw Harry looking at him. Harry held up the towel. He was going to throw it in.

'No!' Wilhelm shouted and blood sprayed out of his mouth. 'No!'

He pushed himself up. His legs were wobbly but he forced himself to stand. He took a couple of steps and raised his fists. Lambert looked surprised and shook his head as if he had decided that the fight was over. But it wasn't.

Wilhelm threw himself at Lambert, his fists pummelling anywhere. Onto the face, into the body. Lambert moved back but Wilhelm followed, punching wildly. He felt pain in his knuckles as they hit bone and teeth but he kept on, stumbling forward with his fists flailing, pounding Lambert. Then suddenly his fists hit air and he almost fell over.

Lambert had skipped beyond his reach. Wilhelm saw the shocked expression on his enemy's face. Saw the blood running from a cut above Lambert's eye, saw the swollen nose and the split lip. Then he heard an angry roar as Lambert darted forward and landed two shattering punches, one to his eye and the other to the side of his head.

For a moment Wilhelm was stunned and his legs nearly gave way, but he swung his fist again. Pain shot all the way up his arm as his fist smashed onto Lambert's chin. Lambert staggered backwards and fell onto the ground. For a few seconds he lay there, then he rolled over and tried to push himself up but his arms gave way and he slumped down again. Wilhelm moved forward, ready to hit him again if he managed to stand up but he felt hands pulling him back. When he looked, Lambert's second had thrown in the towel.

The fight was over.

Wilhelm cleaned himself up as much as possible but he couldn't hide the huge swelling round his eye, the funny shape of his nose and the cuts and bruises on his face. He knew he still looked terrible as he opened the door to his house, but he had a lie prepared. Papa was reading the paper and Mama was at the table. They looked at him as he walked into the kitchen.

'I got hurt at rugby.'

Mama stood up, her hand stretched out towards him.

'*Mój biedny mały chłopiec,*' she said.

82

'I'm not your poor little boy!' he shouted. 'Speak English! Speak English! We live in England, for God's sake!'

He saw Mama's mouth open in shock. He saw Papa drop the paper as he stood up in anger. But it was too late to stop.

'You've lived here for nearly twenty years, so why do you both still talk like Polish peasants? People think we're German spies. That's why no one comes to your bloody shop now.'

'Wilhelm – stop.' Papa's voice was stern and cold. 'You will go to your room.'

He wanted to say more. Wanted to tell them that it was all their fault. But he knew they wouldn't understand, so he went.

Papa came up to his room later and demanded an apology. He refused. And he continued to refuse over the next few days. Finally Papa stopped demanding and a dreadful frostiness fell over the house. Meals were served and eaten in silence. Wilhelm spent most of his time alone in his room.

Going to school was a relief. The fight had cleared the air. Lots of boys in his class patted him on the back the day after the fight and said, 'Well played.' Lambert and his friends ignored him, of course, but everyone else was friendly and seemed to have a new respect for him.

But each evening he had to face the isolation at home.

It stayed like that until one evening when there was a knock on the front door. Wilhelm went to answer it, and for a moment he didn't recognise the man in uniform.

Then the man smiled and ruffled Wilhelm's hair. 'Hello, Will!'

Kristof was home.

The campaign in Gallipoli was coming to an end and the troops were being gradually withdrawn. Kristof had come back with a shipload of injured and sick men.

'And now I've got ten days' leave. I'll be here for Christmas, Mama.'

'God be praised.' Then with a worried look she asked, 'Will you go back?'

'I haven't got the posting yet but it'll probably be France next. Anyway, let's not think of that yet. Now then, Will – tell me all your news.'

Kristof made all the difference. Mama was delighted to see him, and even Papa came out of his gloom and smiled and chatted, although he was still cool towards Wilhelm. Kristof noticed that, and when they were alone together he asked Wilhelm what had happened. It had always been easy to talk to his older brother and now Wilhelm poured out the whole story.

'A fight about our name, eh? I wondered how you got that,' Kristof said, pointing to the yellow patch of bruising that lingered under Wilhelm's eye.

'You should see Lambert's nose – it's still crooked!'

Kristof laughed, then he looked seriously at Wilhelm. 'Papa and Mama are only waiting for a word from you. This bad feeling is hurting them too. You must apologise to them – you know that?'

Wilhelm nodded.

'Good. It's Sunday tomorrow. When we all sit down for lunch would be a good time. Yes? Splendid.'

And that's what happened. As Papa put the joint of meat on the table, Wilhelm stood up and said, 'Papa, Mama – I am ashamed of myself. I said terrible things to you and I am sorry. Please forgive me.'

Papa nodded. 'Thank you. Now it is forgotten.'

Tears brimmed in Mama's eyes as she came round and kissed him on the cheek.

Wilhelm sat down and the weight lifted off his heart. Kristof winked at him.

The next afternoon, Wilhelm looked out of the classroom window during a Latin lesson and saw Kristof walking across the playground. He suddenly panicked – was his brother going to complain about the fight? But Kristof was waiting for him after school and he explained, 'No, I just wanted a look at the old place and see a couple of teachers I used to like. I hear Mr Ward and Mr Sinclair have joined the army – poor, brave blighters. Anyway, the head asked if I'd give a talk at the end-of-term assembly. I don't fancy it much but I said yes.'

Kristof's talk was brilliant – funny and modest and full of really interesting stories. The best one was about how an Australian soldier had invented a self-firing rifle, where water from one tin dripped into another tin which was tied to the trigger of the rifle. When the water in the lower tin reached a certain weight, it pulled the trigger and the rifle fired.

'The Ottoman soldiers thought we were still shooting at them when we were already on our way home!' Kristof laughed.

Everyone loved the talk and at the end the whole school stood and cheered for ages. Wilhelm couldn't stop the silly proud grin on his face, and afterwards he kept telling Kristof how great he had been.

'Hope it didn't sound too exciting,' Kristof said. 'I couldn't say it there, but what happened in Gallipoli is a catastrophe. They call it a withdrawal, but it's a defeat, pure and simple.'

'But we're doing jolly well in France, aren't we?'

'I don't rightly know. But I'm sure of one thing, Will – war is a beastly business. Dirt, disease and death. And seeing friends slaughtered one by one. I just pray the ghastly carnage is over before you're old enough to fight.'

On Christmas Eve, Papa sold only two turkeys and he came up for the evening meal looking very downhearted. But Kristof was on top form and he soon managed to cheer everyone up. He joked and told stories and later he sat at the piano and played songs and got them all singing along. It was the same on Christmas Day. When they got back from church he rushed around helping Mama prepare the meal and then he took Papa to the pub. Wilhelm went with them and stood outside drinking lemonade. When they walked home Kristof was in the middle and he put his arm round their shoulders.

'My father and my brother,' Kristof said. 'I will remember this moment when I'm away at the front.'

In the evening he played the piano again – old songs from Poland – and Papa and Mama sang and danced. And everyone agreed that it was the best Christmas ever.

Then, two days later, Kristof's leave was over.

At the end of breakfast on the last morning,

Kristof said, 'Papa, Mama – there's something I want to say before I leave. I know it would be a big decision but I think life would be better for all of us if we change our names.'

There was a shocked silence and Papa's forehead crinkled in a frown. 'Our name is our name.'

'I know, but Papa, soon you will have no customers, no livelihood, because of the name. And Will has been bullied at school because people think he's German.'

Mama looked across at Wilhelm in surprise. And he nodded to show it was true.

'What's in a name?' Kristof went on. 'Our family history doesn't change if we change our name – only our family's future. Our future is in England – we need an English name. In my unit, I am known as Christopher. It's simpler. I like it when my fellows call me by that name. And it is easy to do – today I'm going to see a solicitor in London before I go back to France and Kristof Linz will officially become Christopher Lindsay. Such a little change, but such a big difference in the eyes of the world. I cannot make you do the same, but I hope you will think about it.'

Wilhelm travelled up to the centre of London with Kristof, wanting to spend every possible minute with his brother. When they arrived at Charing Cross Station another train had just pulled in with hundreds of injured soldiers. Many were lying on stretchers waiting for ambulances to take them to hospital. Wilhelm stopped in shock when he saw one man whose face seemed to have been blown away. Blood was soaking his bandages.

Kristof took him by the arm and hurried him past the rows of soldiers who had lost limbs and men who had been blinded and were standing, lost and alone in all the noise and confusion. A few nurses were trying to cope, but they were overwhelmed by the sheer number of wounded men groaning and crying for help.

'Will, I've got to stay and help,' Kristof said. 'Get back on our train – it leaves in a couple of minutes.'

'I can help.'

'No, go home – that's an order. You'll only be in the way, I'm sorry.'

'What about going to the solicitor to change your name?'

'Helping these men is more important. I'll do it on my next leave. It's only a formality anyway. My friends know me as Christopher, and as far as I am concerned I am Christopher Lindsay already. Go on – run, Will, before the train goes.'

Kristof pulled him close and hugged him and whispered something. Were those whispered words 'I love you'? Wilhelm couldn't be sure because at that moment a piercing scream of agony echoed round the station from one of the wounded men.

'Run!' Kristof said, letting go of him.

Wilhelm dashed down the platform and jumped onto the train just as it started to move. He leaned out of the window and saw Kristof kneeling next to one of the wounded soldiers. Then the train curved away across the Thames and he was hidden from view.

On 20th March 1916, after many discussions and much heartache, Papa took them to a solicitor near London Bridge and they changed their names. Papa and Mama became Henry and Margaret Lindsay, and Wilhelm became William Lindsay.

Papa called in a sign-writer, and soon the shop front proudly read: HENRY LINDSAY, MASTER BUTCHER, and within weeks he started to get more customers. At school, William's form master announced his name change and everyone, even Edwin Lambert, shook his hand.

On 15th July, a telegram was delivered to the house. It read:

WHAT'S IN A NAME

Deeply regret to inform you Cpl Kristof
Linz killed in action France 2nd July.

Later, a letter came from an army chaplain
telling them that Kristof had been killed by
machine-gun fire as he was helping to carry a
wounded man back to the trenches. It added that he
had been posthumously awarded the Distinguished
Conduct Medal.

The day the medal was handed to them, Papa held
it up to show Mama.

'He died with our name, Mama, our old name.'

They always called their lost son Kristof Linz.

But the empty, aching place in William's heart
was for Christopher Lindsay.

THE MEN WHO WOULDN'T SLEEP
Tim Bowler

Author's note

*Writing 'The Men Who Wouldn't Sleep' was poignant
for me. Both of my grandfathers were active in the
First World War and profoundly affected by it, one in
the Flying Corps, the other on the Western Front; the latter
returning with a leg full of shrapnel. Their wives were
affected too and one of them, my maternal grandmother,
lived to the age of ninety-eight and told me many
moving stories about the things that generation endured.
My parents had their own traumas during the Second
World War. 'The Men Who Wouldn't Sleep' is dedicated
to all of them.*

'In war there are no unwounded soldiers.'
José Narosky

I'll never forget the day I met the men who wouldn't sleep. It was the day we heard Father had gone missing at the Somme. Mother sat at the breakfast table in her nurse's uniform and read the telegram in silence, then gave me a small, scared look and turned her head away. I glanced at Molly. She was more interested in her egg than the telegram, but she was only two. She knew Father was in a place called France being something called a soldier and that there was a thing called a war going on, but if she'd picked up from anyone in the village what the arrival of a telegram might mean, she gave no sign of it. I looked back at Mother. She was still avoiding my eyes.

'Mother—'

'In a minute, Robbie.'

'I want to know—'

'Yes, darling, I know you do.' She pushed the telegram into her pocket. 'Listen,' she said, 'I've just got to—'

But she never finished. One moment she was

there, the next she was hurrying from the room. The sound of her footsteps told me she was heading for the conservatory. A few moments later they stopped and in the silence I heard her crying. I looked round at Molly. She'd finished her egg and was now playing with her doll. I kissed her and slipped through to the conservatory. Mother was by the window overlooking the sea. She saw me and quickly dried her eyes.

'Sorry about the tears, Robbie,' she said. 'Won't happen again.'

'Tell me about the telegram.'

'Fetch Nan first.'

But I could already hear Nan's arthritic steps in the hall. A moment later she appeared in the doorway.

'What's happened?'

'Mother's received a telegram,' I said.

'Read it out, Dawn.'

Mother glanced at me and hesitated.

'Read it out, Dawn,' said Nan. 'He's old enough.'

Mother read the telegram aloud. As she did so, I felt something dark lodge inside me, something I didn't have a name for.

Nan spoke. 'It doesn't say he's dead, Dawn. It says he's missing.'

But the dark thing stayed where it was. I stared over the sea towards the distant shore of France, hidden beyond the horizon. It was silent now, but in recent weeks we'd heard a roar on days when the wind blew in the direction of England. People said it was the sound of shells falling at the Battle of the Somme. Pictures of Father were flooding my mind now, but not the ones I wanted. I usually saw him kicking a football with me on the village green, or taking me up on the cliffs to fly our kite and show me where the ravens nest, but now I saw trenches and craters and barbed wire, and smoke and bombs and flying bullets, and bodies and faces, and Father in a blackened uniform, looking like…

'Robbie,' said Mother.

The pictures grew stronger.

'Robbie, sweetheart.' She pulled me to her. 'It doesn't mean the worst. Nan's right. It just says he's missing. We'll get better news soon, I'm sure.'

The pictures remained, but I said nothing. Mother held me tight.

'We've got to be brave, Robbie, all right?' she said. 'Got to stick together and help each other. I know I had a little cry just now, but that was just me being silly and I'm all right now, and you've got to be strong too. It's what Father would want.'

'I know.'

'Good boy.'

She kissed me and let go.

'What are you going to do, Dawn?' said Nan.

'I feel I should go to work,' said Mother. 'There's nothing to be gained by moping around here while we wait for more news, and Dr Bell is so short-staffed.'

Nan's eyes flickered in my direction.

'I know,' said Mother. She looked at me. 'Robbie, I don't have to go in today. I can stay here if you want. But I feel I should help Dr Bell.'

I looked away, the pictures of Father still haunting me. 'I'll come with you,' I heard myself say.

'Are you serious?' said Mother. 'You've never wanted to before.'

'I do now.'

'But why?'

'Because I want to see people who've been where Father is.'

So Mother took me to Blue Water Lodge. A creepy-looking place. I used to be scared of it in the days before the war when Mrs Parrish lived there with her cats, and now that the property had been sold off and converted to a military hospital, I was more wary of it than ever. Mother never talked about her work, but everybody in my class had heard about the man with his face shot away, the man who'd been gassed, the man with both legs blown off, and all the other horror stories. We stopped outside the old iron gates. At the end of the drive, the building rose like a miniature castle. Mother turned to me.

'The men here are in a very bad way, Robbie. Sure you still want to come in?'

I wasn't sure about anything right now – all I could think about was Father – but I nodded.

'All right,' said Mother, 'but if you find it too much, just say and I'll take you straight home. Now, Robbie, one other thing...' She paused, watching me. 'I don't want you to mention the telegram to any of the staff, all right?'

'Why not?' I said.

'I don't want them worrying about us when they should be attending to the patients, and anyway, there's no point just yet. As I said to you before, I'm sure we'll get some better news later. Can you do that, Robbie? Can you keep quiet about the telegram?'

I hesitated, then nodded again.

'Let's go in,' said Mother.

The first thing I saw inside Blue Water Lodge was a naked man. He was curled up in a corner, whimpering, his legs pulled into his chest. A nurse was bent over him, talking softly. Mother led me down a passageway past open doors on either side. Through them I saw bandaged men in chairs or lying on beds, all with limbs missing. I didn't see the man with no face. We reached a door at the end of the passageway and Mother stopped. Through the opening I saw a large room with two men struggling with the help of nurses to walk across the floor.

'The taller man's called Algy,' Mother whispered. 'He was found curled up in a trench, tearing at his own skin.'

'Who's the other man?'

'We don't know. Some of our troops brought him in. He was face down in no-man's-land, no papers, just a German uniform. We've tried to contact the German authorities about him but they don't seem interested.'

The pictures of Father flooded back.

'Let's go outside,' said Mother.

She led me through a side door into the garden. Below me on the lawn were more wounded men, hobbling on crutches or pushed in wheelchairs. I saw a bald man in a white coat hurrying towards us.

'That's Dr Bell,' said Mother. 'I'll introduce you.'

But Dr Bell had no interest in me.

'Dawn,' he said breathlessly, 'I've been looking everywhere for you. We've got an emergency with Sidney. Can you come at once?'

'I've got my son Robbie with me.'

Dr Bell managed a nod in my direction, then turned back to Mother.

'Dawn,' he said, lowering his voice, 'I really need you with Sidney. You're the only person who can calm him down.'

'I'll be all right on my own,' I said.

Mother looked at me anxiously. 'Are you sure, Robbie?'

'I'll be fine. Don't worry.'

I knew she wasn't fooled, but Dr Bell gave her no time to argue.

'Robbie, that's wonderful of you.' He beckoned to another nurse. 'Gladys, this is Robbie, Dawn's son. Can you look after him for a bit?'

'Of course, Doctor.'

And suddenly I was alone with Gladys. She smiled.

'It's nice to meet you, Robbie,' she said. 'Your father's an officer, isn't he?'

'Yes.'

'In France?'

'Yes.'

I turned away, trying to think of another subject we could talk about.

'What happened to the man with no face?' I said.

It was a horrible question, but all I could think of in a hurry. I waited for a disapproving answer but all Gladys said was, 'He died, I'm afraid.'

I thought of the men I'd seen so far, and the ones I hadn't.

'Will many of the men here die?'

'Some will, some won't,' said Gladys. She pointed suddenly. 'See those two?'

I followed the direction of her arm and saw a small hill beyond the end of the lawn. Sitting at the top were two figures, facing the sea.

'The man on the left won't make it,' she said. 'I'll be surprised if he lasts till tomorrow. His friend might pull through.'

'Who are they?'

'The men who won't sleep.'

'The what?'

Gladys laughed. 'It's Dr Bell's name for them.'

'Why won't they sleep?'

'The one on the left can't. The one on the right could if he wanted to, but he's forcing himself to stay awake.'

'What for?'

'The sake of his friend,' said Gladys. 'To be with him at the end. They've been like that for days now. It can't go on much longer.'

I gazed at the two figures. The man on the left was in a wheelchair, his friend on a stool.

'Who's the man in the wheelchair?'

'His name's Jimmy,' said Gladys. 'Strange case.'

'In what way?'

'He doesn't have any physical wounds at all, but it's like he's locked inside himself and can't come out, and now every part of him's shutting down, as though he just wants to die. We're finding more and more men like Jimmy being sent back from the front.'

'What's wrong with them?'

'Some people say there's nothing wrong with them and they're just cowards, but Jimmy's not a coward. He's been broken, Robbie. That's what's wrong with Jimmy and the others like him.'

'Broken by what?'

'The sound of falling shells.'

I stared towards the shore of France. It was still silent, for the moment.

'What about the other man?'

'That's Bert,' said Gladys. 'Stubborn character. Got shot in the leg, then wounded again, but he saw Jimmy quivering on the ground, unable to move, and somehow carried him to safety, and now he won't leave him.' She turned to me suddenly. 'Let's go down and see them, Robbie.'

I felt a rush of panic and stared at her.

'I won't make you if you don't want to,' she said, 'but I just thought you might be able to help Jimmy a little. He's scared of most men, especially if they're wearing an officer's uniform, but a young boy like you could maybe give him some comfort. And he really needs that right now. Will you come with me?'

'I suppose,' I said.

We walked across the lawn and up the path that led to the top of the hill.

'Don't worry if Bert's a bit fierce,' said Gladys. 'He's like that with everybody but he's only trying to protect Jimmy. I promise he won't hurt you.'

'What do you want me to do?'

'Just sit with Jimmy and talk to him,' said Gladys. 'He won't answer. He only ever mutters one word. You'll soon hear what it is. It's the word he uses for the sound of the shells.'

'What am I going to talk to him about?'

'You'll know what to say,' said Gladys.

We drew closer and Bert suddenly turned.

'Who are you?' he said, glaring at me. He struggled to his feet and hobbled behind Jimmy's wheelchair, as though to guard it. He was strong and muscular, but I could see at once that he was in pain. Jimmy did not turn.

'I'm Robbie,' I said. 'I've come to talk to Jimmy.'

'Who says he wants to talk to you?'

'Easy, Bert,' said Gladys.

Bert went on glaring at me, but I could see Gladys was right. He wasn't dangerous. I walked up to the two men, Bert still standing stiffly behind the wheelchair. I stopped beside him.

'I promise I won't upset Jimmy.'

'Talk a lot, don't you?'

'And I promise I'll go away if he doesn't like me.'

'What if I don't like you?'

'I'll take no notice of that.'

'Cocky, aren't we?'

I saw Gladys watching quietly, ready to step in.

Bert grunted. 'Well, you can't do no more harm than Bell's lot.' He nodded towards the stool. 'Sit down, boy.'

'I'll sit on the ground.'

'Sit on the stool, damn you!'

'But what are you going to sit on?'

'Never mind. Sit on the bloody stool!'

I saw Gladys nod and sat on the stool, next to Jimmy.

'Hello, Jimmy,' I said.

There was nothing from Jimmy: no glance, no blink of the eyes. He stared vacantly over the sea, then, after a moment, I saw a flutter of his lips.

'Thunder,' he murmured.

Behind me I felt Bert stir. I looked round and saw him gripping the handles of the wheelchair, his face tight. He caught my eye and scowled.

'I'm sorry about your leg, Bert,' I said.

'Talk to Jimmy. That's what you come for.'

'Did they get the bullet out?'

'They got the bullet,' said Bert, 'but I still got a bucketload of shrapnel in there. They wanted to get rid of it.'

'The shrapnel?'

'The leg, boy.' Bert gave a sudden groan.

'Walk around, Bert,' said Gladys. 'Stretch the muscles.'

Bert stayed where he was, gripping the wheelchair handles. I leaned closer to Jimmy.

'I'm sorry about the thunder, Jimmy,' I said.

As before, there was no answer. Gladys's words came back to me. *You'll know what to say.* I started to talk. I talked about Mother and Nan and Molly, our house, the village, my school. I talked about Norman and Don and my other friends, and some of the things we'd done together, like scrumping in Mrs Howell's orchard, or making catapults, or knocking down ginger at this very house. I talked about everything I could think of except Father. I couldn't talk about Father.

The morning wore on. Gladys slipped away to help an amputee on the lawn. I supposed it meant she thought I was doing a good job, but I knew I wasn't. I was talking about this and that, and Bert seemed to have accepted me, but I was having no effect on Jimmy. His face remained still, and after a while even his lips stopped their murmuring. I peered into his eyes, trying to catch some spark or connection, but all I saw was the unblinking stare. I glanced at Bert, still standing behind the wheelchair, in spite of his pain.

'Is Jimmy hearing me?'

'He's hearing shells, boy,' said Bert, 'the thing he's heard nonstop since the day he went to war.'

I looked back at Jimmy. There seemed no point in talking further. I wasn't helping him. I might even be making things worse. I turned and stared over the sea.

You'll know what to say.

'My father's called Vernon,' I began.

A wood pigeon called somewhere near the house.

'He's mad on football,' I said. 'He's totally crazy about it, Jimmy, like a big kid, but it's good because I'm crazy about football too, because of him, I suppose. He was a really good player when he was younger. Well, that's what he keeps telling me. Mother just gives him that look when he pipes up about how fantastic he was, but I think he must have been pretty good because he's got lots of trick shots and things when we kick a ball around together.'

The sea was growing paler, more still.

'We often go and watch matches together,' I went on, 'but we haven't been for a long time because of the war. The last big game he took me to was the FA Cup Final back in 1913. Do you remember that one, Jimmy? Father wanted Sunderland to win because Villa have won it loads of times, but it was a terrible match. The ref was useless. He kept stopping the game because of fights between the players, and then Charlie Wallace crossed the ball and Tommy Barber stuck it in the back of the net, and Villa won one–nil. Father thought Sunderland could have had a chance if the ref had been better.'

The wood pigeon called again. I stared at Jimmy's face, but as usual, nothing moved in it. I tried to think of something else to say, but it was no good, and after a while I gave up and just sat there. Around the middle of the day Dr Bell came down with a chair. Mother was with him, carrying a tray with glasses of water and bowls of soup. Bert looked up with a scowl.

'Who's that chair for?'

'You,' said Dr Bell.

'Do I look like I need a chair?'

'You do, my friend.'

Bert ignored him and touched Jimmy on the shoulder. 'Bit of soup, mate?' he murmured. 'Going to get some down this time?'

Jimmy said nothing, his stare more fixed than ever.

'He don't want none,' said Bert, glancing at Dr Bell, 'and neither do I. The boy can have it.'

'I don't want any either,' I said. I saw Mother frown and added, 'Thanks, anyway.'

Dr Bell seemed unconcerned and simply took a glass of water round to Jimmy and eased it between his lips, keeping a handkerchief underneath. It was hard to tell whether Jimmy drank anything, but Dr Bell went on trying, then after a while he wiped Jimmy's chin with the handkerchief, stood back and turned to me.

'Thanks for helping out, Robbie,' he said. 'Why don't you take a break now and spend some time with your mother? She's free for the next hour.'

'I'm staying with Jimmy,' I said.

Dr Bell glanced at Mother.

'Robbie's fine,' I heard her say.

And a moment later I was alone again with Jimmy and Bert. I didn't bother trying to speak now. I knew there was nothing useful I could say. Jimmy was fading so fast I wondered if he even knew I was there. He just sat there motionless, Bert standing behind him as before, ignoring Dr Bell's chair.

In the late afternoon, I heard a groan. 'I'm not going far, boy,' said Bert, 'and remember – I'll be watching.' He gave me a hard look, then stomped back to the lawn and started limping about to stretch his leg.

I watched him for a while, then turned back to Jimmy. He was probably no older than Father but he seemed so ancient. I wished I could have done something for him. I stared down at the ground, the pictures moving in my head again.

'We had a telegram this morning,' I murmured.

The dark thing inside me, the thing I had no name for, felt heavier.

'That's why I'm in a state,' I said. 'It was about Father, you see. I didn't tell you earlier but...he's an officer in France and...he's been fighting in the Battle of the Somme, and the telegram says he's gone missing, and Mother's being brave and saying everything's going to be all right, and we'll get some good news soon, but the thing is, Jimmy...'

My mouth felt dry. I tried to swallow but couldn't.

'The thing is, Jimmy...I just know he's not coming home.'

I heard a sound behind me and turned to see Bert hobbling back. He reached us, glowered at Dr Bell's chair for a few moments, then collapsed into it. As he did so, I felt Jimmy take my hand. I looked at him, startled, but nothing else had changed: the still face, the unblinking eyes. If anything, he seemed more remote than ever. I looked down at his hand. It was bony but strong: the hand of a man growing old too quickly.

An hour passed, another. We sat there in silence, the three of us, Jimmy's hand still holding mine. At some point in the evening I realised Dr Bell was standing behind us, with Mother and Gladys. Someone put a blanket over Jimmy's legs. I leaned closer to his face.

'Has the thunder gone now, Jimmy?' I whispered.

His hand grew cold, but I didn't let go. For some minutes, no one moved, then Dr Bell walked slowly round, checked Jimmy's pulse, and eased my hand free. Mother took it at once. I peered up into her face.

'I know what's happened,' I said. 'We've had another telegram.'

She nodded gravely. I looked past her and saw Nan standing on the lawn. She too was grave. Molly was beside her, hopping and skipping on the grass. She saw me and came running over, laughing. I stepped away from the others and picked her up, but she was already staring past my shoulder.

'Why's that man crying?' she said.

I saw Bert turn his head away. I kissed Molly.

'Let's go home,' I said.

'Can we come back tomorrow?'

Mother walked over and took Molly from me. I looked back at Jimmy. His body was slumped forward and Dr Bell and Gladys were bending over him.

Bert thrust them aside. 'I'll carry him in, not you.'

'Can we come back tomorrow?' Molly said again.

I caught Bert's eye, daring me. I looked at Jimmy, now in his friend's arms, and Father's face floated before me.

'We'll come back tomorrow, Molly,' I said.

As we walked away, I heard the thunder start again across the sea.

DANDELIONS FOR MARGO
Linda Newbery

Author's note:

*I've written novels set during the First World War
and have always been interested in the work done by
women and girls, and the difference it made to their lives.
I hadn't yet written about the Land Girls, and this
anthology gave me the chance. The title came from
picking dandelion leaves for my friend's tortoise.*

It was the fourth summer of the war. And, for Lizzie, the summer of the Land Girls.

It was also the summer of Margo. When Tom came home from training camp, just before he left for France, he gave her to Lizzie as a birthday present.

'Chap in the pub was selling them. He had a dozen of them in a sack. They're Greek, he said.'

Lizzie gazed at the tortoise in fascination – at her shell marked in rounded squares of rich ambers and browns, and at the glimpse of scaly legs and strong claws. The tortoise was firmly inside her shell and that was all that could be seen.

'What use is *that* as a pet?' Dad humphed. 'And how do we look after it?'

'We'll find out. I'll get a book from the library.' Lizzie was delighted; this was the best present she'd ever had. 'I'm going to call her Margo.'

'Funny name for a tortoise,' said Mum. 'And how can you tell it's a she?'

That was a good question, but since she had no way of knowing Lizzie decided to think of the tortoise as *she*, and to keep the name. Margo seemed just right, especially when the tortoise ventured to stretch out her neck and nibble at a piece of tomato.

There was a kind of elegance about her. She had a wise, scaly face, bright little eyes and tough claws that clicked on the lino as she walked in her strangely determined way. Before long Lizzie was sure that Margo could recognise her, and knew when her name was called.

Tom left for his train to Dover and his ship to France. Dad made a little house for Margo from a wooden crate, with a mesh run attached. For winter he found a smaller box in which Margo could hibernate when the cold weather came. Lizzie read all about it, with the deep pride and responsibility she felt a tortoise owner ought to have.

The Land Girls, across the road at Home Farm, were Helen and Josephine. The family already knew Helen, who was the doctor's daughter and had gone away to Ashford to become a suffragette. Mum disapproved of Helen, calling her *hoity toity* and *above herself*. She'd said that when Helen rode about on her smart pony, and even more when Helen wrote letters to the local paper about Votes for Women and handed out leaflets in the street. 'What do they want the vote for?' Mum had tutted. 'Why can't they leave well alone?'

Helen had been doing some kind of office work, but now she was back, working on Mr Baynton's farm. Other young women drove ambulances or worked in the munitions factories, but Helen was a country girl with the skill to handle Hercules, the big plough horse. There were officers billeted at the doctor's house, so she was living at a hostel in Ashford, and cycled to the village every day with the other girl, Josephine.

Mum had disapproved of that too, at first. 'Girls on bicycles! Girls wearing trousers! Whatever next?'

But the war was making lots of things seem normal. The girls wore tough breeches, close-fitting to the knee and baggy above, like the ones army officers wore. And bicycles were by far the best way of getting about – quicker than walking, and easier than waiting for a lift in a van or a cart. Lizzie watched the girls coming and going, laughing and calling to each other as they rode along the narrow lane. One day she'd try to get a bicycle of her own.

Before the war it would have been Tom going over to the farm every day, and coming home late and tired. At first it seemed that he'd stay there, because England at war still needed farmers. It was after seeing Helen in Ashford with a recruiting poster that he'd changed his mind.

We don't want to lose you, but we think you ought to go…

Nothing Helen did could make Mum feel any more warmly towards her. Mum blamed Helen for

Tom joining up – even though, since conscription had come in, he'd have been called up anyway. Mum's latest complaint was, 'All those young madams thinking they can take over men's work! What'll be left for the men, when the war's over?'

But when would that be? No one knew. It wasn't finished by the first Christmas, like everyone had said. Nor by the second Christmas, or the third. And no one was saying that it would be over by *this* Christmas.

Thomas had gone, and Oscar too, his best friend, who'd been Dad's apprentice in the smithy. Dad worked on his own now, with just his collie Maisie for company, but it didn't matter because most of the horses had gone to the war too. Only a few ponies and the farm horses were left.

Lizzie would always remember the first time she met Josephine.

The sun slanted low through the elms as she picked dandelion leaves for Margo from the grass verge. She heard their voices first, on the farm track, laughing and calling to each other. Helen was in front, pedalling vigorously – she was energetic in everything she did. The other girl, a little way behind, seemed to be struggling, wrenching the handlebars to steer her cycle round hard-baked ruts.

Lizzie called hello to Helen, but it was the fair girl she was more interested in. She had heard about Josephine from Tom, and knew that she lived in Ashford, and was Oscar's sweetheart. According to Tom, Oscar talked about little else but Josephine since he'd met her at an Easter fair. 'Mind you, she *is* pretty,' Tom had said, then added, 'No, pretty doesn't tell you the half of it. Lots of girls are pretty. Josephine – well, she's…'

Lizzie was devoted to Oscar herself, having looked up to him for as long as she could remember. Sometimes she had hung around the forge to watch him work. He was strong and capable, but so gentle with the horses, his big hands calming the most skittish or nervous ones. Secretly, she even dreamed of being his sweetheart herself when she was grown up. So, waiting for Josephine to come into view, she was ready to be resentful, half hoping to find her ordinary, or stuck-up, even ugly.

All that changed the moment Josephine drew level. She tilted her bicycle, awkwardly astride, as if it were an unpredictable horse that might buck her off at any moment. She was gasping a little, and hot, and a sticky strand of hair stuck to her forehead. But nothing could dim her extraordinary beauty.

Helen had already stopped. 'What have you got there, Lizzie?'

'Dandelions. Dandelions for Margo. She's my tortoise.'

'Tortoise!' Helen said, laughing.

'You can come and see her if you like. She's in the garden.'

'Perhaps another time. We're tired and thirsty. We're going to the Horseshoes for cider and supper. Jo, you don't know Lizzie, do you? Tom's sister.'

'No.' Josephine wobbled a bit in her saddle, and smiled. 'Hello, Lizzie.'

And that was all she said before they waved and rode on, but later, getting ready for bed, Lizzie could remember the exact tone and pitch of her voice – rather low, and quiet.

Lizzie didn't keep a diary, but often thought she needed to, for times when something special happened. Like the day Margo arrived. Like today. Lizzie didn't think she'd ever seen anyone so...so... she didn't even know what word was needed. Not just pretty. Not just beautiful. Josephine seemed to be made of different stuff from ordinary people. She was taller and slimmer than Helen, with long corn-coloured hair held back in a single pigtail underneath her brimmed hat, and dark brown eyes. Perhaps it was that unusual combination – fair hair, dark eyes – that made her so striking. And golden skin, dusty from working in the fields, her nose a little reddened with sunburn. Her smile was like – well, like a blessing. That was the only way Lizzie could think of it. Josephine seemed quite unaware of how dazzling she was, how no one could help gazing at her.

No wonder Oscar loved her. How could he not? And probably, Lizzie realised, Tom did too.

It must be fun, she thought – working on the farm, talking and laughing together, cycling to and fro. Drinking cider at the Horseshoes! Whatever would Mum say about that?

Next morning the post office boy came to the door. Dad was at the smithy, so it was Mum who answered.

Lizzie had been clearing the dishes from breakfast but now she stopped and gazed out of the window. She thought her heart had stopped. Everyone knew what it meant when the post office boy cycled along the street, bringing a telegram. Last July there had been twelve houses in the village with closed curtains and blinds because the soldier of the family had been killed in the Big Push. And there had been more drawn curtains since then. Poor boy! People called him the Angel of Death.

But this time he wasn't.

When Mum came back into the kitchen she looked as pale and shaky as Lizzie felt. She gave a hesitant smile.

'It's from Tom! He's coming home on leave. He'll be here by Sunday.'

Mixed up with Lizzie's gladness was a feeling of guilt, because she had promised herself that she'd think about Tom every single day, think really hard, to help keep him alive and safe, not dead in a grave somewhere in France, like Dollie Bates' brother or Andrew Smith's father. But some days she'd forgotten. How could she? Some days she hadn't thought about the war at all. It had been going on for such a chunk of her life, it seemed. It took something startling, like the bombing raids on London or the death of a someone from the village, to claim her attention.

She went into the garden and lifted Margo out of her run – carefully, supporting her underneath, like the library book said you should. Margo stretched her neck and looked around hopefully.

'I mustn't forget again,' Lizzie whispered. Because if she did, and something bad happened, it would be her fault.

Lizzie often dawdled on her way home from school as she passed the fields of Home Farm. She hoped to see Helen or Josephine, or both of them, in their breeches and shirts and broad-brimmed hats, out working. Mornings and evenings they milked the cows, but in between they were usually outside. If they were near enough they came over to chat.

They still hadn't come to see Margo, but once Josephine helped with the dandelion-picking. While they chose the best leaves, she asked Lizzie what she wanted to do when she left school. Lizzie replied, 'I want to work in a zoo,' and because that sounded silly she asked, 'What about you? When the war ends, I mean?'

Josephine sighed. 'All I really want is to marry Oscar. You'd better not tell Helen I said that. She's all for women having careers of their own, not just wanting to be wives and mothers.'

'Do you really think women will get the vote?'

'Helen says we will. She says we won't give up till we do.'

Walking home on the last day of term, Lizzie thought of the summer holiday ahead. Mum would want her for jobs at home, but also, when she could, she'd help Helen and Josephine with their farm work. It could be her own war effort – hard, sometimes, but more fun than knitting socks. She was sick of socks, having knitted till her fingers were sore. Since war broke out she must have produced enough socks to kit out a whole platoon, if they didn't mind the lumpy toes.

Mr Baynton and the girls had been working hard

to get the barley in. As she turned the bend in the lane from the village, Lizzie saw the dark brown bulk of Hercules coming through the gateway, pulling the hay cart into the field where barley had stood tall until this week. She had liked the look of it: the bearded golden stems rippling in the breeze like newly-washed hair. Now the field looked bare and shaven. Just a few stooks remained at the lower end, by the stream. The wheat would be harvested later.

A cloud of dust rose from Hercules' big hooves and from the wheels of the cart. Usually it would be Helen holding the reins, but this time it was Josephine who sat in the driver's seat. Helen must be busy somewhere else.

Lizzie saw Josephine looking round anxiously to make sure the wheels didn't scrape the gateposts. When the cart was safely through, Lizzie raised her arm and waved extravagantly, hoping Josephine would see her against the hedge. Josephine waved back, and called a greeting.

At the same moment Lizzie became aware of another sound – a buzzing drone, like a huge insect. She craned her neck to see. The drone was louder – coming close, very close. Then she saw an aircraft, wavering in flight, narrowly missing the farmhouse chimney. A cry caught in her throat.

It was a Gotha bomber. She'd seen them before,

like huge clumsy dragonflies, often harried by the smaller British fighter planes as they made their way to London. This one was alone, and in trouble. Its wings dipped one way and then the other, and a stream of black smoke trailed behind. It had come so low that she could see numbers and letters on its sides, and the stark black German cross. It was going to crash, surely!

The engine noise became a stricken roar. She glimpsed the pilot's head as he struggled for control. For a second she thought it would plunge into the field right in front of her. She smelled the smoke, hot and acrid. The pilot must have made a last supreme effort. The Gotha rose, barely clearing the trees by the stream, and floundered on too damaged to stay airborne. Nose down, it wavered towards fields beyond the village.

It was too much for Hercules. Lizzie became aware of a crisis closer at hand. The big horse had reared in panic; now he ran back, and slipped down between the shafts of the wagon. She saw Josephine jump to the ground.

Lizzie ran across the stubble. Dimly she registered the sound of smashing and explosions a few fields away. But someone else would have to help the Gotha crew, if they were still alive to be helped.

Hercules was trying to struggle to his feet, but

had a hoof over the rein, holding his head down. On the ground he was a mountain of a horse, hairy hooves flailing, sides heaving. Lizzie saw his ears flat back, his eye rolling in fear.

'Whoa, boy, whoa—' Josephine's voice was full of alarm. She wasn't used to horses. With shaking fingers she unbuckled the rein from the bit.

Freed, Hercules flung up his head, striking her hard in the face; she fell back with a cry as the horse heaved himself to his feet. Slowly she raised a hand to her eye. Lizzie saw the trickle of blood, then more as it splashed into the grass.

What to do first? Steady the horse, or help Josephine?

'Jo! Jo!' Helen was running fast down the slope.

Kneeling, Josephine lowered her hand and looked in dismay at the blood.

'It wasn't Hercules' fault. He didn't mean…'

'I know, I know. Shhh, I'll take care of you.' Helen put an arm round her and examined her face, smoothing away the hair with gentle fingers. 'It's your eyebrow that's bleeding. Not your eye.' She pulled a handkerchief out of her pocket and held it to the wound.

'I feel sick,' Josephine said indistinctly.

'Yes, I expect you do. Sit down for a minute. Lizzie, can you take Hercules back to the stables?'

Hercules was looking a little self-conscious. He gave himself a good shake, snorted, and began to crop grass. Lizzie refastened the rein so that she could lead him.

'Yes. Of course I can.'

All the talk in the village was of the crashed Gotha, and the deaths of its crew of three. The pilot and one of the gunners had been killed in the explosion, and the third died of terrible burns soon afterwards.

'Still, they were Germans,' said Lizzie's mother, at home that evening. 'They started it. They deserve whatever they get. You won't catch me weeping over dead Germans. You know what they say. The only good Jerry's a dead Jerry.'

Lizzie did weep, in bed. She kept going over and over the horrible thrill of seeing the stricken Gotha, knowing it must crash, and that the poor German airmen were doomed. And she thought of Helen supporting Josephine as they walked back to the yard, Josephine leaning against her with a handkerchief clamped to her eye, not enough to stop the blood from splashing over her shirt and her breeches.

Josephine was away from work for two days. Lizzie helped Helen to bring in the remaining stooks of barley and to feed them into the threshing machine.

Mr Baynton was there too, working the machine; he wouldn't let the girls do that. 'We don't want another accident.'

'It was my fault,' Helen kept saying. 'I shouldn't have let her drive the hay cart on her own. She wanted to, that was the thing, and Hercules is always so good.'

Mr Baynton was brisk. 'She'll be fine, now they've sewed her up. She's a good strong lass.'

Would Josephine have a scar from the stitching? Lizzie hoped not. She couldn't bear to think of Josephine's lovely face being spoiled.

None of this was as awful as the news about Oscar.

It was Dad who heard first. Oscar's home was in the next village and his mother had sent his uncle to tell Dad and show him the telegram, because Dad had been Oscar's boss, and had known him well.

Oscar had been in no-man's-land mending wire in front of the trench when he was killed by a shellburst. He'd died instantly, the telegram said.

Oscar's mother had written a note to Dad, asking him if he'd let Josephine know.

'How can I do that?' Dad came straight indoors to tell Mum and Lizzie. 'Poor young girl – what will I say?'

'She'll have to know. And – what about Tom?'

Mum wondered. 'He must be on his way home.'

Lizzie felt too numb for tears. Oscar. Lovely, kind Oscar, with his gentling hands and his way with the horses. Gone. She'd never see him again. None of them would. He'd never again come whistling into the forge, greeting Maisie as she bounded up to lick his face.

Maybe it was a mistake. Maybe it was someone else who'd died, and Oscar would come home on leave with Tom, the two of them filling the kitchen with their big rucksacks and their laughter. Because, of course, Oscar must come back, to marry Josephine. It was the only proper ending.

As it turned out, Dad didn't have to tell Josephine what had happened. He and Lizzie walked to the farm after lunch and found Helen on her own, mending the fence by the cows' water trough. Lizzie could see that Dad was mightily relieved to pass on the information and head back to work, leaving Helen to break the news.

It was a dismal homecoming for Tom, even though Mum had made a special dinner, with mutton stew and apple pie.

He did know about Oscar, and told them more. 'It was the night before I left. I was carrying sandbags up from behind the line, and when I got close to our front I heard yells and knew something had happened. They called for a stretcher-bearer, but it was no use.' He stopped, and bent down to bury his face in Maisie's ruff. 'He was killed outright,' he said, after a moment. 'That bit was true, any rate...I – I saw. Can't believe it. Don't think I ever will. Good old Oz, my best mate. You'd think I'd be used to it by now, people getting killed, but it's like this is the first time.'

'Oh, Tom.' Mum kept reaching out for his hand across the table, as if she couldn't quite believe he was there unless she kept touching him.

What if it's Tom, next time? Lizzie thought.

It mustn't happen. She mustn't let it. When he went back she must think of him, hard, every morning and every night, last thing.

To cheer Tom up, she took him into the garden to see Margo. She lifted the tortoise out of the run and made sure he held her properly.

He admired the brightness of Margo's eyes, the cleverness of her look. 'I can see you're looking after her.'

'Oh yes, I do! Do you think she's grown? *I* think she has.'

'Maybe.' Tom held the tortoise carefully, but soon handed her back. 'Here. Her shell makes me think of a Mills bomb. I don't want to hurt her.'

Lizzie didn't know what he meant, but she took Margo and stroked the top of her head. 'When the weather starts to get colder I'll feed her up as much as I can, so she's ready to hibernate. Dad's made a special box, so she can have a nest of hay. I've read all about it.'

'She's lucky.' Tom looked wistful. 'I wish I could hibernate.'

'Till the war's over? I wish you could, too.'

Later, after the cows were milked, Tom went over to Home Farm to talk to Josephine. Lizzie knew that he wanted to tell her good things about Oscar, how popular he'd been in the platoon, how brave; things for them both to remember.

Lizzie went out too, for dandelions. It was a warm evening, the light only beginning to fade. Swifts screamed high in the sky, fast as arrows. They'd soon be gone – when autumn came they were first to leave, before the swallows and the house martins.

The two girls were about to cycle home. When they saw Tom coming along the track they waited for him, and Lizzie saw their heads close together as they talked. After a few moments Helen mounted her bicycle and rode up the lane to Lizzie.

'Thought I'd leave them alone for a minute.'

'Will Josephine be all right?' Lizzie asked.

Helen turned and looked back. Josephine and Tom were both standing with heads bent, talking quietly. Josephine had pulled out a handkerchief and Lizzie could see from the jerking of her shoulders that she was crying. She wore a padded bandage under her hat, over her stitches.

'I think so,' said Helen. 'Eventually. I'll look after her.'

Lizzie thought of Tom going back to France, and of all that might happen over there. Her heart clenched with fear. She had somehow imagined that *special* people – like Oscar, and Josephine, and Tom – would be safe, because it was what they deserved. Now she saw that the war would take whoever it wanted. The war didn't care. It was strong, huge, ravenous. It could swallow people whole or spit them out in bits, and no one knew how to stop it.

All she could do was wait, and hope.

'Here, I'll help.' Helen dropped her bicycle into the verge and they picked dandelions together, not speaking. Tom and Josephine had started to walk slowly towards them, still talking in low voices, Tom pushing Josephine's cycle.

The dandelions on the verge grew thickly. Some had bold yellow flowers; others bore pale round seed-heads, the dandelion clocks children puffed their breath at, making the individual seeds float away on the air. When Lizzie bunched the leaves in her hand and tugged, the plant resisted for a moment then gave way, a length of white root coming up with it. She put the whole plant into the basket for Margo.

But she knew that part of the root was still left underground to grow again. It was strong, undefeated. It would push up again soon, making a new rosette of leaves, and flowers like bright little suns.

There would always be dandelions.

THE BROKEN PROMISE
Malorie Blackman

Author's note:

I wanted to write a small, personal story about two half brothers set against the horrific backdrop of the Great War. It was really interesting to do the research so I could get the details right. I considered doing a submarine story, or one about a suffragette going to work in a munitions factory, but I finally plumped for an underage boy swept up by his enthusiasm of the war until the grim reality of it sinks in.

Dear Grandad,

Try not to die of shock at me writin to you. Well - we have moved yet again. I am not alowed to say where to but I will have to brush up on my parly vous. We are dug in nice and snug but from time to time Fritz make a nusance of himself. I cannot complain to much because I am with a grand bunch of lads, and we all muck-in together. You know what thats like - a bit like a campin trip - except everybody has a gun - ha ha!

This will all be over soon - so at least Titch will not have to come here when he's older and get all muddy! As soon as we give the Hun a bloody nose, I will be home to. Say hello to Titch for me and tell him that I'm not missing him at all. Ha ha!

Cheerio,
Dan
P.S. Ta for the socks

Of course, that were just Danny being Danny. He didn't want to have any fuss. I might have only been fourteen but I weren't completely daft. In his younger days Grandad had been a soldier so he knew what was what, and even I knew The Great War weren't a campin' trip, not by a long chalk. I could tell from Danny's eyes on his leave that he'd been through the mill. But still, I wanted to do me bit. I needed to. It just weren't right, me brother fightin' over there while I stopped at home, tucked up safe in bed like a bairn.

So, one Saturday morning, I told Grandad I were going fishin', but instead I went down to the local recruitin' station and I stood in line with a big crowd of other men an' waited for over an hour.

And when it were my turn I went in and stood in front of the recruitin' sergeant. There were an officer there too, he looked familiar but he said nowt. He were just standing off to one side havin' a cup of tea.

The recruitin' sergeant gives me the eye.

'How old are ye?' he asks.

Now that was a bit of a problem for me. Although Danny called me Titch, that were only because he were a giant! I were a good five foot six, so I were fine on that score. But I weren't exactly sure how old you had to be – some said it were eighteen – but I was as sure as I could be that fourteen were too young!

'Eighteen!' says I with a straight face.

He looks me up and he looks me down, and his eyes get a bit narrow like. 'Eighteen, eh?'

'Aye, eighteen!'

It's dead quiet for a bit, wi' just the tickin' of a big wall clock, an' he's staring a hole through us, and I know that I'm going to get rumbled. I can feel the officer starin' too, an' he strolls round to sit wi' the sergeant. I know they're goin' to ask for me birth certificate or somethin', and then I'll get sent home wi' a flea in me ear.

And then I work out why the officer is familiar. It's Richard Armitage, the doctor's son. He's been away at university for a good few year now, but before that he'd been friendly wi' Danny. He'd been round our house loads of times. So that's that! Richard knows me, and no amount of tryin' to look grown up will change that. I'm a coloured lad and practically everybody else in town is white.

Me heart's goin' like it wants to jump out me chest but Richard still says nowt. And then the sergeant just says, 'Good lad!', and he sticks out his hand and I shake it. I can't believe it! The sergeant looks down and starts to write on me papers, and then Richard leans in an' says something in his ear.

I'm sunk! It took a while, but the cat's out the bag now. The sergeant looks back to me, and then takes up his pen, and he draws a line through what he's just written and then he writes somethin' else. I don't know exactly what's goin' on, but Richard suddenly stands up and starts to stroll out. And as he passes me he smiles an' says, 'Well done, Billy.'

And that were that. I took the oath to serve King and Country and I were in. Private William Archer, a soldier for three years, or the duration of the war, whatever were longer.

As I were walkin' home, I felt eleven foot tall. I felt like I could fly. I told Grandad what I'd done, and after a moment's silence he nodded and clapped me on the back. He were like that, never said that much, but I could tell he were proud.

Apart from Grandad and Danny I didn't have any other family. Me mam had died havin' me, and then when I were six me da got killed when a steam engine exploded at his work. Funny, that. Grandad had been to Africa and survived battles with the Boers, but me da died in a factory in Darlington.

Me mam's family were all blacks. Her parents had both been slaves in America but they'd escaped. Grandpa Joshua, he's me mam's dad, had joined up wi' the North Carolina Coloured Volunteers and fought for the Yankees in the Civil War, and Grandma Ruby had been smuggled away to Canada when she were a bairn. Years later, they met up an' had me mam Harriet.

Me da's family were all white, though. He were married to a wealthy lass called Louise and they had a son. That were me brother, Danny! But then she died o' diphtheria, and Dad had to go over to Canada to sort out some business. That's where he met me mam. He married her and fetched her back to England, and that's when I were born. So me and Danny were only half-brothers, but that seemed to work pretty much like real brothers. Some days we got on, most days we were at each other's throats. All brothers rub each other up the wrong way sometimes, but me and Danny had more reasons than most.

Every time Grandad separated us, he'd say, 'You two can fight like two ferrets in a sack, but just remember, family always comes first. Brothers are supposed to look out for each other.'

'He ain't no brother of mine,' Danny muttered.

First time he said that, it hurt. I admit it. Twentieth time he said it, it still hurt. As far as me brother was concerned, I was just someone he had to put up with.

I weren't the only dark 'un in town but there weren't that many of us. I used to get some name-callin' – you know, 'Pickaninny' and 'Teapot' – an' most o' the time I let it go. Sticks and stones an' that! But if anybody got too nasty, then I'd clock 'em one. Or at least try. And if they were too big, or if there were too many, then Danny would step in and sort 'em out.

'He's my responsibility and no one gets to duff him up but me.' Many a bully got to hear that line before they got a good hidin' off Danny for pickin' on me when I were a nipper! But I always got the feelin' that Danny were stickin' up for me 'cos he had to, not 'cos he wanted to. The blokes he were thumpin' were the blokes he should have been matey with, but he were always scrappin' on account o' me. Some funny beggar would make some crack about 'biscuits left in the oven too long' or 'Billy boy, couldn't yer dad find a white lass to wed!' and I'd start a ruck and Danny would get roped in. But as I got older, getting' on for ten or eleven years old, I started clockin' 'em for meself and makin' it count more often than not. And Danny got less keen on jumpin' in for me.

'You'd better start learnin' to get along wi' folks,' said Danny. 'I'm fed up lookin' out for you all the time. You're not a bairn any more.' He never actually left me in the lurch, but you could tell he was mad at me even while he was cloutin' some big-mouth.

One day, I were comin' back from buying some candles for Grandad when I saw a big crowd o' lads coming up the hill, on their way to play football at Skelly Bank.

'Can I play?' I shouted, friendly like.

'No!' shouts one. 'Get lost.'

'Darkies are useless at football,' shouts another.

'Darkies are just useless,' adds a third.

And then they all pitch in with their tuppence worth. Well, so much for sticks an' stones! Two seconds later I were like a windmill, all swinging arms. Me against the world. No surprise that I were gettin' a pastin' off them. But suddenly Danny were there. He must have heard the commotion 'cos he came flyin' out the house and started steamin' in. And now we're both getting a hammerin', but we're gettin' some licks in too. When Grandad arrived, swingin' his walkin' stick and cussin' fit to shame the devil, the footballers ran off!

Danny an' me were a sight, all swollen eyes and split lips, but we'd stood our ground.

'Thanks,' I grinned to him as we cleaned ourselves up at the pump.

He glared back at me o'er the horse trough. 'Are you soft in the head?' he demanded. 'There were ten or more of 'em.'

'They called me names. And they said I were useless!'

'God, I wish we weren't kin.' Danny gave a disgusted snort and shook his head. 'Titch, you'd better start usin' yer brain and stop getting' yerself in trouble 'cos this is the very last time I'm gonna help you when you get yerself in bother. That's a promise.'

And with that, he marched back indoors.

Me and Danny had lived with Grandad ever since Da died, at least until Dan joined up in 1914. Dan had got himself into some scrapes with the police an' he were findin' it difficult to get a job, so as soon as England declared war on Germany an' the call went out for volunteers, he were off like a rat up a drainpipe.

And now it were my turn.

The next few weeks were actually great fun! For a start, from the minute I shook that recruiter's hand, I felt part of something, not so much on the outside any more. I knew I'd done the right thing, that I was doing me bit. I were following both me grandads into the army. I got given a uniform and put in a barracks with some other chaps. They worked us hard but I didn't mind that. We ran and jumped and lifted logs until we got fit, and we marched up an' down all day long while a holy terror of a drill instructor called McMurtry shouted the odds. Some of the other fellows carped a bit about all the square-bashin' and said that McMurtry was worse than the Hun. They didn't see the point of the spit and polish and the paradin' up and down, but Grandpa had explained it to me a bit so I knew what it were about.

'Sometime it'll seem like stupidness,' he said. 'And you'll feel like clockin' someone for bein' bossy for no good reason. But it's all about bindin' you men together as a team an' to get you used to followin' orders. When yer in't thick of it, when you've got Huns all over you, doin' what yer told can save yer life.'

We were taught how to handle a rifle, and how to make sure we hit what we wanted to hit – and didn't hit anything else! And we practised fixin' bayonets on the end of our rifles and chargin' at potato sacks while screamin' like banshees. And we learned about concealment, and how to advance usin' cover and a hundred other bits and pieces that a soldier needs to do his job.

And then, just like that, the thirteen weeks of trainin' had flown by and we crammed into a train headed down south to Folkestone. Next we took the ship for Boulogne. It were meant to take about two and a half hours, but the weather was that bad it took five! I swear we went up and down more than we went forwards. Some of the chaps were green and havin' a terrible time, hangin' over the side and bein' sick and all, but it didn't bother me a bit. I'd never been on a boat before but I thought it were a grand laugh. I even had a spot of lunch.

* * *

When we arrived, France didn't look that different from England. Green fields, nice little villages with churches and little shops and some pretty lasses wavin' at us. And there were hundreds of men in uniform everywhere. There were differences of course. I couldn't speak a word of the lingo but that wasn't that big a problem because we didn't get to talk much to the locals. The big difference was the wounded. You couldn't help notice the number of men with bandages, or walking on crutches, or bein' carried back to the port in ambulances and lorries. It might sound daft but that's the first time it felt like a war. You know, with people getting hurt. Up to then it had just been grand fun and gettin' fit an' learnin' to shoot. But these chaps had been in a real scrap – and they weren't all goin' home.

We spent another couple o' weeks trainin' and then we got moved up nearer the front. We were all excited to be going up to the line, but I were double excited. I might get to see Danny again for the first time in months. And then suddenly I felt a bit queer. What if he weren't there? How did I know that he hadn't been wounded and already sent back home to Blighty? What if he were... No! I forced meself not to think on that.

We were slated to stay back in reserve, but after a few days, some of us got word that we were movin' up to the front to fill in some gaps. There were no guarantee that we'd see any action but we'd be a lot closer to it!

As we got nearer the front, we started to see huge piles of stores piled up. Feed for the horses, shells for the big guns and mile after mile of horses and lorries loaded wi' stores an' ammunition. But as well as that, you could see a change in the people. The folk were still friendly, but they weren't so jolly. And lookin' at the shell holes in the fields, and the ruined buildings you could see why.

We'd only just arrived in the support trench, and we were waitin' for someone to come back and tell us where to go when Danny walked in. My brother, Danny. I were flabbergasted. What were the odds of that? But then I wondered if maybe Richard Armitage had pulled a stroke back at the recruiting station and fixed it for me to get posted wi' Danny? Anyroad, I were that glad to see 'im that, even though he hadn't seen me yet, I nearly made a fool of meself by runnin' over like a three-year-old when 'is dad comes home. Dan looked tired but fit too. And he had stripes up! They'd made him a corporal!

I wasn't sure what to say or do so I kept still, grinnin' like a ninny.

He turned, and when he saw me his face fell, like I were a ghost come back to haunt him.

'Billy? What the hell are you doing here?' he asked.

Me grin vanished. 'I joined up,' I said, like he hadn't already worked that out for hisself.

'But you're...' His voice trailed off and he looked at me like I'd arrived just to torment him. Now he'd have to suffer all the comments again, and explain how he had a darkie brother. The look on his face were that unhappy, I thought he might clock me one. In that moment I realised that Danny would never see me as family, not proper family. I were just the nuisance he was forced to share a house with.

'Sorry, Danny,' I muttered.

'Corporal!' he snapped. 'You call me Corporal. We're not up Skelly Bank now.'

'Sorry, Corporal.' I straightened up and looked him in the eye. I wouldn't forget again. No family, no expectations.

Unexpectedly, his face softened. 'You never could stay out o' trouble, ya daft beggar,' he said. 'C'mon. Stow yer kit over there, an' I'll give you the royal tour.'

He took the four of us new blokes in tow and showed us our sector on a map, an' pointed out where we was and where the Hun trenches lay, barely a hundred yards away across no-man's-land. He took us from the support trench to the reserve trench, and then right up to the front line. I had a look through a periscope but there were nothin' to see. None of the Germans were daft enough to stick their heads up for us to shoot at. After that, we had a bit of time for a brew and a chat. We were in a tiny dugout off the support trench where Danny bunked wi' three other NCOs, and we were enjoyin' a bit of chocolate that I'd brought.

I noticed Danny had a souvenir Luger, taken from a dead German. Compared to the old-style cowboy six-shooter that our officers carried, the Hun weapon looked sleek and modern. I picked it up. The grip looked to have a funny angle to it, but it felt really comfortable in me hand. I sighted down it, shootin' an imaginary Hun wi' it.

'Yous'll have to excuse 'im,' Danny said. 'He'll be six next birthday.'

The other chaps laughed, and I blushed and put the pistol back on his pack.

'How did you two meet up?' Corporal Higgins asked.

'Meet up?' I started. 'We're—'

'So, Billy, what do you reckon to life at the front?' said Danny.

I just looked at 'im. He'd cut me off that quick, it couldn't have been any clearer. He didn't want anyone knowing I were his brother. He'd got away from havin' a dark 'un in the family, an' now he didn't want to go through all the awkward questions again. There were a big fat silence. Everybody knew that somethin' was up, but they didn't know what.

'Well, Corporal, it's not too bad,' I said at last. 'Nice and dry, at least!'

The others all snorted. 'You wait till the rains come, son!'

Danny stayed pretty quiet, but I got a lot o' good tips from the old stagers, little tricks of the trade that made life a bit easier. Then it were time to get back to the rest of me section. As we were comin' out the dugout, a stretcher party come past carryin' a wounded man. They'd cut his trousers off, and he had a big bandage on his leg but he didn't look too bad. He were half sittin' up, smokin' a Woodbine as the two bearers laid down the stretcher.

'Well, Smudge,' says Danny, 'I heard you'd copped a Blighty One.'

'Looks like it, Corp, looks like it,' said the chap on the stretcher. And he reached up to shake hands with Danny. 'Mind how ye go, son.'

'God bless,' said Danny as the two orderlies picked up the stretcher and moved off down the trench.

'What's a Blighty One?' I asked, once they were out of earshot.

'It's a wound that's not bad enough to kill ye, but bad enough to get ye sent home to Old Blighty.'

After that, many was the time Danny tried to get me on my own to talk to me but I avoided him like the plague. I'd got the message, it didn't need repeatin'. A week went by without very much happenin'. I don't know what I expected really. We'd had officers tell us what life was like at the front during training, but it were still strange to be here. We didn't have to do any square-bashing, of course, but then there was no canteen either.

From time to time some Hun sniper would take a pot shot at our lines but that weren't too much of a problem as long as you remembered to keep your head down. But some days the sky was so blue and it were so quiet that you could forget that there were a war on.

One night, about one in the morning, four of us were chattin' in a support trench when this captain appears out of nowhere, bustles up and says, 'Evening, you chaps. I have to run a little errand and I need someone to watch my back. Come along!'

And he leads us out into the night. I've got no idea where we're goin' but we head off down the support trench, up a communication trench to the front line and then up into a sap that led to a forward listening post. I'd never been so close to the Boche before. The sap was a half-finished trench that stuck out into no-man's-land, pointing like a finger at the Hun lines. I swear you could hear them breathing. It were black as a badger's bum when the moon went behind the clouds, and I kept looking up, expectin' to see some Hun towerin' above me ready to drop a grenade on us.

I don't know what the captain was doing but I felt naked as a new-born out there. When he wanted to speak, he'd bring his mouth so close that I could feel his bristly moustache ticklin' my ear! He were movin' some wooden boxes about like he were playing draughts wi' them, and from time to time he'd get us to carry one for him while he fiddled wi' another.

But then, out o' the quiet and the blackness comes a voice – a German voice! There's a pause, and then all hell breaks loose. I dunno if they come deliberate or if they was patrolling in no-man's-land an' got lost in the dark, but suddenly they've dropped into our sap and we're sharin' a trench wi' a Hun patrol. I drop the captain's bloomin' box and go for me rifle, only it's several yards away. I'm tryin' to get to it when the moon slides out from behind a cloud and I'm face to face with a Hun – a skinny lad same age as me, with eyes big as saucers. But he's got his rifle.

It's not snug into his shoulder like for taking careful aim – he's carrying it low – but when he sees me he lets one off.

I'm dead! I think.

But I'm not. Somehow he's missed me – from three feet away! His eyes get even bigger and he looks down and starts to work the bolt on the rifle so he can try again, but he's so close I grab the end of it and pull. And then we're going at it, rollin' on the duckboards, scrappin' like two mangy dogs over a bone. He knees me hard in the stomach. I double over and stumble backward, landin' on a pile of tools that have been left in the sap. The Hun boy picks up his rifle and works the bolt – he won't miss again – but I scramble up and swing a shovel, and it hits him just above the ear. He goes down, his eyes still open like he's surprised. And there's a sticky black stain like tar on his head. But it isn't tar, it's blood, black as hell in the moonlight.

I throw up. Maybe it's the excitement, or the fear, or maybe it's that the dead Boche reminds me o' me. Suddenly Danny's there, checking the Hun. Then he turns to me, his face grim.

'You hurt?'

I shake my head.

'Are you sure?'

I nod.

'Where's yer rifle?'

I still can't speak and he shakes me hard. 'Where's yer gun?'

I point up the trench.

Danny slaps me across the face, so hard my teeth rattle.

'You *never* get more than arm's length from yer gun. Not ever! Ye hear me? Never!'

He fetches me rifle and thrusts it back at me like he's trying to plant it in me chest, just as the captain and the other two return, and together we slip back to our front-line trench.

Later, I sit in the dugout and look at my hands. They're shaking – and I can't seem to stop them.

A few days later, we found out why they were stockpilin' all that ammunition. We were goin' on the attack. The fight with the German lad in the sap had been nasty but I hadn't had time to think. It all happened so fast, I just got stuck in before I knew it. But this were different. This were planned. All of us knew we were going over the top. And once our artillery opened up on them, even the Germans would know. When the barrage stopped, we'd be crossin' no-man's-land and then the serious dyin' would start.

Some of the lads made bad jokes, and some made

noises like 'it's about time' and 'now we'll give the Hun a taste of his own medicine' and rubbish like that. Me? I didn't joke, or say anything. I just went off me grub, and got more an' more scared as the days went by. Fifty times a day, my mouth went from as dry as cold ashes to spit constantly fillin' it up. I was too afraid to even close my eyes. But eyes open or eyes shut... I couldn't get the look on the Hun boy's face when I'd hit him with the shovel out of my head. And the truth of it is, I envied him. He was out of it. I wasn't. Home had never seemed so far away.

Come the day, and we were all stood to. It were still dark, but no matter 'cos I hadn't slept a wink. Ladders had already been propped up against the parapet of the front-line trench to let us climb out, and we were all standin' and waitin'. There were mostly silence in the ranks, apart from some sniffin' and someone who kept quietly clearing their throat, but nothin' dramatic. Everybody was grim-faced, mouths dry. I saw Boxer trying to whistle, but his mouth weren't working and his lips kept twisting into strange shapes. The lieutenant checked his watch for the fiftieth time. I reckon that, despite all the jolly pep talks, he were as scared as the rest of us.

The idea behind the barrage sounding around

us was to cut the barbed wire and to soften up the Hun trenches. It were terrifying enough for us, and we weren't the target. It were the Boche getting pasted today. At least, that were the plan. But Danny had told me that it didn't matter how hard you knocked the Hun, they just kept their heads down till you stopped shelling them and then they popped up again.

A trench never smelled good at the best of times, but right then it smelled like a bog-house. The old sweats used to joke that that's why we wore khaki trousers – so you couldn't see the crap – but nobody was laughin' that morning.

Even though it was bloomin' freezing, I felt so unbearably hot, I could hardly breathe. Me heart was jumping around in me chest like a trapped rabbit. I was on the verge of bottlin' it – too scared to stay, an' too scared to run. If I went over the top, the Hun'd kill me, but if I didn't, me own mates would shoot me.

And then the shellin' stopped and there was a sudden silence. Not the good silence that meant somethin' had ended, but a terrifyin', gut-wrenchin' silence that meant somethin' much worse was about to start. A whistle blew. Lieutenant Cantley-Troubridge was already on the bottom rung of a ladder.

'Here we go, chaps! God speed!' He started to climb out the trench.

The men followed him up the ladders, but I was still flappin' like a headless chicken. I'd dropped me rifle and when I bent to pick it up, it wouldn't stay in my sweaty hands. I heard the Hun machine guns open up, and I heard screams comin' from no-man's-land. Screams like nothing I've ever heard before. Screams that ripped through me worse than bullets because they didn't stop and wouldn't stop and I could feel each an' every one.

I dropped to me knees in the middle of the trench an' I opened me mouth and started to scream too. The trench was nearly deserted now. Danny grabbed me by the scruff of the neck. He knew I was thinkin' about boltin' and he got me up against the back of the trench. He started shouting at me but I couldn't make out what he was sayin'. What did it matter what he was sayin'? The last man went up the ladder and now it was just me an' Danny. He was still shouting at me but I still couldn't hear it.

I was drownin'.

I was bein' buried alive.

Danny shouted right in me face but I still couldn't hear any words. Danny reached down and picked up me rifle and shoved it at me so I had to grab it, and then he shoved me up the ladder. I tried to turn to go back down, but the bayonet on his rifle pressed into me and I had to go up. I reached the top and I couldn't see nothin' for the smoke. Danny was behind me, shoving me toward the Hun trenches.

We'd only gone about twenty yards when Danny pulled me down into a shell crater. I lay on my back in the shell hole and I didn't know what was going on. Maybe I'd died already and this was hell. There was the crack of rifle fire going over my head and the rattle of machine guns and the sound, oh, God, the sound of screams. All I wanted was to run back to our trench and then back to the depot and then back to England, except now I didn't even know which was the way to our lines. I was going to die in a hole in France. I looked across at Danny, me eyes pleading.

I was five years old again, and gettin' bullied, and I needed me big brother to jump in for me. Except this time there was nowt he could do. He stared at me, his face a mask. What was he thinkin'? Resentment? Pity? Disgust?

He laid his rifle down across his legs, reached inside his tunic and pulled out his souvenir Luger. What was he doin'? What use was a pistol here?

His gaze was still pinning me to the shell crater floor as he slowly raised the gun and pointed it straight at me. A moment of confusion, and then I got it. Danny was goin' to end me. He was goin' to put me out of my misery like a knackered horse. And I couldn't say I blamed him. I'd been nothin' but a problem to him for years.

I closed my eyes, tears pricking at my eyelids.

There came a loud bang and a hot, searing pain shot up from me foot and into me leg. And just like that, calm and quiet fell over me like a blanket.

This was it!

I was dead or dying.

I thought of Grandad. At least Danny had made sure I died in battle. I was just grateful that it weren't a firing squad.

Bloody hell, but it hurt. Being dead or within spitting distance of it shouldn't hurt so much! I opened my eyes and looked down. There was blood on me boot.

What the…?

Danny dropped the Luger and came over to me. He tied a belt round me leg just above me knee and wound it tight to stop the bleeding. He clapped a field dressin' on me foot and all the time I gawped at him like an idiot.

'I don't understand. I thought you was— Why didn't you…?'

He picked me up by my webbing and shook me hard until I stopped yammerin'. His face is only inches away from mine.

'Yer hurt,' he said, 'but it won't kill yer! D'yer understand?' He shook me again. 'Titch? Do you understand?'

I nodded.

'Now stay down! Just stay here until a stretcher-bearer comes for you.'

'I'm useless. Go ahead and say it,' I said bitterly. 'Why didn't you just take the chance to do what you've always wanted and get rid of me for good?'

'You're not useless, you big twit. You're only fourteen, for God's sake. I've seen grown, hardened men break down and bawl at the sound of guns.' Danny looked at me for a moment, then he smiled, a sad, resigned smile. 'You always were a daft beggar but you're me brother an' family. I've been trying to tell you that for the last little while.' He gave me a tight, fast hug. 'Remember to keep yer head down, Billy boy.'

An' wi' that he turned around, picked up his rifle and vaulted out of the shell hole to run and catch up wi' the other blokes on the attack.

'Danny!' I shouted. 'Danny!' But he was gone.

I stayed in that hole for a long time. It were dark again before they found me and pulled me back to our trenches. I lost the leg. The medics said that sixteen hours were too long to have a tourniquet round a leg. So by the time they took it off, me leg had gone bad and they had no choice but to cut it right off. But I didn't blame Danny for that. He weren't a doctor, he were just doing his best. If it weren't for Danny I'd have been cut down by the German gunfire or else I'd have run away and got shot as a deserter. Danny had given me my 'Blighty One'.

Danny died that day. So did the rest of my platoon. I don't know the details, but the Germans buried them. I was a fourteen-year-old boy, still wet behind the ears, who should've died too.

But I didn't, because my brother Danny broke his promise. I look back and it fills me with sadness that it was only in that last moment in the shell crater that I realised just how much my brother loved me.

GRANNY MEASHAM'S GIRL
Adèle Geras

Author's note:

When I was asked to write a story for this anthology, the one thing I knew was: I was going to keep well away from all battlefields, mud, trenches and the like. I am much more interested in those who stay behind and are left to cope with the fallout from the conflict.

January 1915

Elsie Measham would rather have stabbed herself with her own knitting needles than admit to being in love. She looked around her at the thick white walls of the little church, noticing the carved angels at the end of every pew and the sun making spots of colour where it shone through the stained glass and told herself that maybe she was wrong and she wasn't in love after all. Being in love was something that wasn't supposed to happen to you when you were only twelve. Elsie knew this because her granny had said so, not so long ago. When Phyllis from the smallest of the farm cottages became engaged to her sweetheart before he went off to the war in France, Granny was quick to pass judgement.

'Lot of nonsense, this love business,' she'd announced to Elsie last October, while stirring the pudding for the Shelbrooke family Christmas. 'Phyllis can't be a day over sixteen. How can she know her own mind? And her Jim's no more than a boy. I was the one who cured him of the croup.'

Elsie hadn't uttered a sound and simply stood by to hand her grandmother the currants when she needed them. She didn't say, as she might have done: 'But you were married at sixteen, Granny. You had

165

your first son at seventeen and were widowed by the time you were twenty-five.' It didn't do to contradict Granny Measham, especially when she was stirring something or otherwise occupied in the kitchen of Shelbrooke House preparing food for the family upstairs.

That Elsie was permitted to be in the kitchen at all was a privilege and an honour. She had only just left school and over and over again, Granny had made it quite clear that it was a very lucky girl indeed who was taken on to help in Shelbrooke House. 'You're welcome as long as you're a helping hand. Once you become a naughty little girl, I'll send you packing.'

'I'll be a helping hand,' Elsie said, and she'd kept her word so well that everyone in the kitchen, in the butler's pantry and everywhere else this side of the baize door that separated the family from the servants, had grown quite used to her presence. She'd been working in the big house for two months, and everyone called her Granny Measham's Girl. Oh, Granny Measham's Girl can bring the eggs in from the larder. Send Granny Measham's Girl to fetch cream from the farm. Granny Measham's Girl can carry a tray of tea things if she's careful. Granny Measham's Girl is a dab hand with the knife when it comes to peeling potatoes. And so on and on.

The vicar – round, cuddly-looking Reverend

Burchin – was in the pulpit and Elsie knew by the way the silence felt that the time was drawing near for the reading of the names. This was the worst part. The congregation knew who from the village and the surrounding area had been killed since the last list was read. The names had gone up outside the post office and the families had been told, and had wept privately, but here in church everyone knew who they were and it was hard not to stare at them when the names were called. Everyone tried to be brave, of course but you could hear muffled sobs and see shoulders heaving and hands trembling and the whole thing was dreadful and Elsie wished, as she wished every Sunday, that she hadn't come.

I should have stayed knitting in the kitchen, she told herself. But she knew that she couldn't do that. Granny was in church and her place was at Granny's side. Also, and this was even more important, she needed to come to church to pray for Piers, Lord and Lady Shelbrooke's son who was far away fighting. Elsie felt that her prayers might be the one and only thing keeping him safe from harm. She bent her head and repeated the words she'd been saying over to herself every Sunday since the war began: 'Dear God, please keep all our brave soldiers safe but especially Piers. Especially dearest Piers.'

The sermon was boring. Poor Reverend Burchin

did his best, but his voice was like a lot of bees buzzing and Elsie did what she always did while he droned on and on: she daydreamed. Today she was remembering the first time Piers had ever spoken to her. He was in bed with a chest infection.

'Poor lad can hardly breathe,' Mrs Hughes the housekeeper told them all in the kitchen. 'Doctor says he mustn't stir out of bed. Not even to eat his breakfast.'

So Ann, one of the maids had gone up to the bedrooms with a tray. When she came back to the kitchen, she said to Granny: 'You forgot the toast rack, Mrs Measham.' She was out of breath. Granny said: 'Next thing, I'll be forgetting my own apron. Elsie, Ann's tired out...you take the toast rack up. You know where Mr Piers's bedroom is, don't you? Next door to the Lilac Room.'

Elsie fled, carrying the toast rack as carefully as if it was a bag of precious jewels. She knew where everyone slept. Mrs Hughes had taken her round the house properly when she first started to work there and shown her everything, though of course, she knew the downstairs very well. She said, 'It's no good not knowing what's what. Not if you're here to help your granny. You never know when you'll need to run an errand.'

On that first tour of the house, Elsie marvelled at

the richness of the curtains, the softness and colour of the rugs, the height and grandeur of some of the beds, which were crowned with draperies and swags of velvety stuff. The chairs were upholstered in brocade. The light fittings were gilded. Everything looked as though kings and queens could live here. She said as much to Mrs Hughes, who laughed when she answered: 'Oh no, this is nothing but a simple country gentleman's house. A rich gentleman, to be sure, but no king or queen in this family.'

She thought of those words as she knocked and opened the door to Piers's room. He looked about as far from being a prince as Elsie could imagine. He was lying back on his pillows with his eyes almost closed and she nearly dropped the toast rack when he spoke to her.

'It's very kind of you to bring my toast. Especially as I don't think I'll eat it.'

She couldn't help herself. She said, 'I do think you ought to eat it, you know. It's very good for you. It'll help you get strong and well again.'

He sat up then and looked at her. And then he smiled and Elsie felt as though someone had taken her heart and squeezed it. Piers was beautiful. His eyes were as blue as the curtains at the window. His face was pale, because he wasn't well, but she wanted him to smile again and then he did, and she knew that she would collect and keep those smiles in her memory and go over them at night when she was alone in her tiny bed under the eaves. They would be her private treasures.

Elsie stopped remembering the day she first met Piers and came back to where she was: in the church, listening to Reverend Burchin who showed no sign of stopping. Elsie remembered the black day, the day Piers set off for the war. She'd wanted to wail and cry and tear her clothes with misery but she couldn't because what she felt for Piers was her secret. Still, as she stood with the other servants, watching Piers in uniform striding off to the railway station, accompanied by his father, Lord Shelbrooke, she found one tear sliding down her cheek and had to wipe it away with a corner of her handkerchief.

On the night that Piers left the house to go to France, she said to Granny Measham, 'Can I do some knitting?'

She knew Granny would be pleased. After all, she'd been the one to teach Elsie. 'My best pupil,' she always called her. 'Much better at it than your poor mother ever was.'

Elsie hadn't known her mother. She'd been taken, that was the way Granny put it, years and years ago and Granny was the only mother Elsie could remember. But when she asked if she could knit, she knew exactly what she wanted to make: a long, thick, woolly scarf. She would knit love into every single stitch and magic as well, and when Piers wrapped it round his neck it would keep him safe and warm and snug and he'd have to think of her making it, every single time he touched it.

March 1915

That was only two months ago when Piers was still alive and when she could still hope to see him again. Now, on another Sunday, walking back from church to the house in the snapping wind, Elsie kept her eyes on the ground and missed entirely the sight of the first daffodils at the side of the road. Spring could hang glory from every tree but a fat lot Elsie cared about all that. She was thinking about how different the big house was now from what she was used to. She sometimes wondered what Piers would have thought about the changes, but since that black and hideous day when the news came of his death, her head was packed full of sorrow and she found it hard to think about anything very much.

Lord and Lady Shelbrooke seemed, when she saw them in church, to be shrunken imitations of the people they used to be. Lady Shelbrooke's eyes were red-rimmed always, though none of the servants had seen a tear fall. She must weep all night, Elsie decided, when no one's about. Lord Shelbrooke's gaze was fixed constantly on his shoes, where once they glared fiercely about the church, as if, Granny Measham used to say, 'he was marking us all off on a register, to see if we're attending properly to the service'.

The house had been turned into a rest and recovery home for soldiers. Days of moving furniture about; of setting out rows of beds in the biggest rooms downstairs; of making sure the doctors' and nurses' accommodation was prepared to an adequate standard followed the announcement, and Granny Measham had her hands full with the catering.

'Family is one thing. Parties is another, but I've never in my life had to cook for scores of convalescent men. They'll need feeding up too, if they're to recover.'

Elsie was needed as never before. She ran about the whole day, fetching and carrying anything anyone wanted moving about. She helped the scullery maids prepare vegetables in large numbers. She helped the gardeners plant what needed to be planted. She dusted where she was told to dust. What she never did any longer was knit. Piers's scarf, as she thought of it, was pushed into an old pillowslip which Elsie kept in the bottom of the chest-of-drawers in Granny Measham's cottage. She was trying to forget about Piers and the knitting was a terrible reminder. Every night, when she said a prayer for him in heaven, she thought she'd unravel the scarf and give the wool back to her granny, but she couldn't bring herself to do it. Every row held a memory of Piers. She wouldn't have been able to remember nearly so much from looking at a ball of crinkly wool.

'Dr Davies is waiting for you in the ballroom,' said Ann, coming out of the kitchen and catching Elsie before she'd even hung her hat up. 'Best hurry.'

What can he want with me? Elsie wondered. She raced through the rooms till she came to the ballroom which was now more like a hospital, with beds lined up against the two long walls with a space left clear between them so that everyone else could walk up and down: the nurses, the doctor and any servants with trays of food and now Elsie herself.

'There you are, Elsie,' said Dr Davies, who was tall and skinny and had a face like a friendly bird. His hair was dark and soft, like feathers, but it often stuck up because of his habit of running his fingers through it. He was standing at the end of one of the beds. 'I wonder if you could do me a favour? This is Douglas. He's lost one of his feet, poor chap, but doing very well on the whole, aren't you, Douglas?'

Elsie looked at Douglas in the bed, and he nodded. He looked quite small for a soldier, and didn't seem old enough to have had a foot shot off. She closed her eyes and tried not to think about that too much but to listen to what Dr Davies was saying.

'Douglas comes from Scotland and it's anyone's guess how he ended up here. Of course, we're doing what we can to get him moved to a place nearer his home, aren't we, Douglas?'

Douglas smiled weakly and muttered something. 'But meanwhile,' Dr Davies continued, 'he needs a bit of cheering up. I thought of you, Elsie, because you always look so cheerful. Do you mind chatting to Douglas from time to time? Perhaps reading to him, or something? How would that be?'

Elsie didn't know where to look. *Why me?* she thought, but she couldn't say it. Instead she said, 'Yes, Doctor.'

'Capital, capital,' said Dr Davies, and without another word he strode off down the corridor between the ranks of beds to go and attend to someone else. Elsie was left staring at Douglas and hadn't an idea in her head about what to say to him.

'What's your name?' Douglas began. 'The doctor didn't say.'

'Elsie Measham,' said Elsie. 'My granny is the cook here.'

'Food's very good,' said Douglas. 'You can tell her that.'

'I will,' said Elsie. What next? What could she say? She wasn't going to mention the foot. Every time she thought about that she felt ill. She looked down at the blanket where it covered his legs and shivered.

'How old are you?' Douglas said, and then, 'Come and sit here. On the chair.'

Elsie sat. The chair was hard and she didn't know what to say. How were you supposed to cheer someone up?

'Don't worry about that doctor. He's far too keen on everyone being happy in this room and it's hard. You ought to hear us sometimes…it's shrieks and sobs and Lord knows what at all hours of the night. Stands to reason really.'

'But it's sad that you're so far from home,' Elsie said. 'If I was wounded, I'd want my granny to come and sit with me. Have you got a granny?' *There*, she thought, *I'm chatting to him. It's not so hard, after all.*

'A granny, a mother, no father, and a sister almost exactly the same age as you are. How old are you?'

'Twelve.'

'So is she…Marie. That's her name.'

What to say next? 'I wish I had a sister. Or a

brother, I wouldn't mind that either. There's only me and Granny. But of course,' she added, 'I'm perfectly happy on my own.'

That wasn't quite true, because of Piers and how much she thought and dreamed about him, and how horrible this war was, but Elsie wasn't going to say she was miserable. What were her troubles compared with this poor young man losing his foot and missing his family?

'I know why the doc sent for you to talk to me,' Douglas said. 'He caught me last night.'

'Caught you doing what?' Elsie asked.

Douglas looked down at his hands which seemed to have a life of their own, plucking at the edge of his sheet, folding it over, and then picking at it again. He turned his eyes on Elsie. They were very dark and the veins in his forehead showed blue under his white skin.

'Crying,' he answered at last. 'I never cry. I haven't cried since I was a bairn. I didn't even cry when that happened.' He nodded towards the end of the bed and smiled. 'Well, I fainted from the pain, so I couldn't and then they gave me all sorts to drink so...'

'Crying's nothing to be ashamed of,' Elsie said. 'I cry all the time.'

'But you're a wee girl!' Douglas said. 'Begging your pardon, Miss Elsie.'

'Just Elsie. And I am not "wee",' she added. 'What made you cry last night?'

'I got a postcard from home. It reminded me… well, it was a photograph of my family, so…'

'Will you show it to me?' Elsie asked. 'I love photographs. Is Marie in the picture?'

Douglas nodded and reached for a book that lay on his bedside cabinet. 'Here,' he said, and held out the postcard.

'She's pretty!' Elsie said. 'What a beautiful postcard. I like her boots very much.'

'She looks like you, a little,' Douglas said. 'I think that was why the doctor thought you might cheer me up.'

'I'm nothing like her!' Elsie frowned. 'Whatever do you mean? She's dark and I'm mousey, she's very slim and I'm…not. She has beautiful boots and I don't…she's not like me a bit.'

'She's looking straight at me out of the photograph and her eyes are clear and honest. She's not hiding anything. She's not smiling falsely but simply gazing at me. You're not a smiler for nothing, either. I've noticed that.'

'When did you notice that?'

'Now. While we've been talking. You don't smile for no reason. I like that in a person.'

'Perhaps I ought to smile more, if I'm supposed

to be cheering you up.'

'Well, perhaps, but I'd prefer it if you only smiled when you felt like smiling. Not on my account.'

Elsie couldn't help smiling at that. She was finding it quite easy, after all, sitting here next to Douglas and talking about nothing very much. Down in the kitchen, Granny was probably wondering what had happened to her; why she wasn't there to give a hand with the serving out and taking of trays to various parts of the house.

'Would you like me to read to you? That's what Dr Davies said I might do.'

'If you like. Later on, maybe. But tell me some things, first. About this house. About the Shelbrookes. It's kind of them to allow their home to be turned into a hospital.'

'They've lost a son,' Elsie said. 'Do you know that already? Piers, his name was. He died quite a short time ago...everyone's very sad, of course, but his mother most of all, I think. Lord Shelbrooke can't show it but he's heartbroken.' As she spoke, Elsie saw that this was true. 'Piers was only twenty. Is that how old you are?'

'I'm nineteen,' said Douglas. 'I was longing to go over there and fight. I thought it would be...' He closed his eyes. 'An adventure.'

Elsie said nothing. She'd heard enough, from

gossip below stairs, from whispered remarks by everyone in the village, to know that the death and destruction were terrible. Hell, people said. The worst hell you can think of. Mud. Blood. Dead bodies. Bits of people hanging on barbed wire. Horses dying too. Awful, awful things that Elsie heard about and tried at once to forget, though that wasn't easy. She wasn't going to ask Douglas about his foot, or about what happened to him in France. No.

'Did you and Marie have adventures together?' She had no idea whether a brother who was seven years older than his sister went adventuring with her. She tried to imagine how it would be if Douglas was her brother. What sort of things would they do together? Much more than Piers, he seemed the kind of person who might be a companion in some games; a person who'd go for walks in the country with his sister and take her to the fair. Were there fairs in Scotland? And did his family live in the town or in the country? She knew nothing of Douglas's life.

'Aye,' Douglas said. 'I did a lot of looking after her when she was small. I had to take her around with me. I didn't like it a lot of the time, but my mother worked at the bakery round the corner so it was down to my gran and me...'

* * *

'What's that?' Douglas pointed down at the bag sitting on the floor by Elsie's feet. A week had passed since she first came to talk to Douglas.

'My knitting,' she said. 'Do you mind if I do some knitting while we talk?'

'No, of course not. I didn't know you could knit.'

'Granny taught me.' Elsie took out the half-finished scarf she'd put away when Piers died.

'Who are you making it for?' Douglas asked. 'It's already quite long. I like the colour, like leaves in the autumn.'

'No one,' Elsie said. After a moment she added, 'No, that's a lie. I started it for Piers Shelbrooke. Everyone was knitting things for the soldiers so I wanted to make something for him. Then he died, so I put it away. But last night I thought I'd like to start it again. It's silly for such good wool to be stuck away in my chest–of-drawers, isn't it? When someone can make good use of it.'

'That's true. It would be a shame. You go ahead and knit. It's soothing to watch. My gran knits all the time. I used to help her wind her wool.'

Elsie had been coming to Douglas's bedside every day for the last week and they were now good friends. She no longer found it hard to think of things to talk to him about. They took turns reading aloud to one another from *Alice's Adventures in*

Wonderland which was Douglas's favourite book. Time passed very pleasantly, but you couldn't read aloud the whole afternoon.

'Your turn,' said Elsie. 'I want to know what happens when Alice visits the Mad Hatter. And I want to knit now. It's such a long time since I've done any.'

April 1915
Elsie had been suffering from a bad cold and Dr Davies had banned her from the ward, which was what he called the ballroom. She had to stay in the cottage by herself, and what else could she do but knit? She'd finished the scarf and there it was, wrapped in brown paper and ready to give to Douglas as a gift when she went back to the house. How surprised he'd be, when she told him it was for him! Elsie, when she was on her own, found that she thought about Douglas rather a lot. What she felt for him wasn't what she had felt for Piers, and maybe neither feeling was what older men and women thought of as love, but maybe this feeling of friendship and affection was truly love and perhaps what she'd felt for Piers had been something else. A sort of adoration. She enjoyed talking to Douglas. They laughed together. He'd cheered up tremendously since Elsie had come along, Dr Davies

said, looking pleased that he'd had the idea in the first place.

When she arrived in the kitchen, Granny Measham said: 'Well, you're looking smart and a good thing too. Dr Davies was asking for you. They're off to the station in an ambulance and can't wait...'

Elsie flew up the stairs and into the hall where she could see Douglas, in a wheelchair, with some of the other patients standing around him. She knew what that meant: he was going home. He was well enough now and she should have felt happy for his sake but she wasn't happy, not at all. To her horror, she felt tears starting to come into her eyes. Douglas was wheeling himself across the black and white tiles towards her and she made an effort to pull herself together and, above all, not to cry.

'Elsie! I'm going home...can you credit it? They're sending me to Scotland...there's a nurse taking me all the way on the train. I'm going home.'

'That's good,' Elsie said and stopped. She didn't trust herself not to burst into tears if she spoke too much. Then she said, 'I'll really miss you, Douglas,' and wondered at her own courage.

'And I'll miss you, Elsie. Ever so much. You've been a real pal.' He took Elsie's hand and squeezed it and Elsie thought she was going to faint. 'But we'll write, won't we? Here, look, I've written my ma's address on a card for you. Please write. Promise?'

Elsie took the card Douglas held out to her and put it in her overall pocket. He wanted her to write to him. Perhaps he wouldn't be lost to her for always. Perhaps they'd meet again. Elsie's thoughts ran and skipped and leaped in her mind, over the years, over the time when she was still a girl to when she'd be a woman; someone who could go where they liked when they felt like it. She'd fly to Douglas's side and they'd renew their friendship only it would turn to true love and they'd be married and have lots of beautiful children...

'I promise. Every week. I'll write to you every week. Will you write to me too?'

'Not every week, I shouldn't think! But as often as I can.'

'I've got a going-away present for you. Here.' She thrust the parcel into his hands. 'It's the scarf. The one I've been knitting. I know it's warm now but...'

'Not in Scotland. April in Scotland is very cold sometimes. I've known snow to fall...' He took the parcel and tore off the paper. The scarf, looking like a carpet of autumn leaves, unrolled and fell down past his knees to the marble floor. Douglas picked it up and wound it round his neck. 'It's a marvel, Elsie. I will wear it every day even in the hottest sunshine.'

Elsie laughed. 'Don't be silly,' she said. 'You must put it away in mothballs in the summer.'

'I will. I'm teasing you.'

The doctor was calling Douglas. 'I have to go,' he said. 'I want to say…there's so much I want to say. But most of all, thank you. You really did cheer me up, Elsie.'

She couldn't have said, later, how she came to be so bold. But Douglas was leaving and perhaps it would be years till she saw him again. She leaned over and kissed him quickly on the forehead. He put out a hand and squeezed her on the arm.

'Goodbye, Elsie. Till we meet again.'

Elsie waved as the wheelchairs and the walking patients left the house. She turned and went back downstairs to the kitchen where Granny Measham was waiting.

'Where've you been?' she asked.

'Saying goodbye to Douglas,' said Elsie.

'Douglas this, Douglas that…' Granny muttered. 'You've been nothing but Douglas for weeks. Much the best thing for him to go home if he's well enough. Now, you come and see about these spuds, my girl. They won't peel themselves.'

Elsie took up the knife and settled down in front of a huge bowl filled with potatoes. She had never thought of writing to Piers and wished that she'd had the chance to tell him how much he meant to her. She would never have dared to ask anyone for his address, but now she began to compose in her head the first of her letters to Douglas. She could feel the shape, in her overall pocket, of the card with his address written on it. *Dear Douglas*, she thought. *Dear Douglas…*

THE MURDER MACHINE
Oisín McGann

Author's note:

When Tony approached me to write a story about Ireland during the First World War, I was delighted for the chance to take it on, but realised that it came with a great deal of responsibility. Irish soldiers in the British Army endured the trauma of the First World War, only to return home and face the upheaval of the Irish War of Independence, which in turn led to a bitter civil war that divided the country. Writing the type of thriller storyline that would grab young imaginations, while paying proper respect to the people damaged by these conflicts, proved to be a huge challenge, but I hope I've succeeded.

The first man Jimmy Reilly ever saw killed was his father. As Jimmy settled into a fitful doze, his dreams brought him back there again, to the moment when the soldier kicked in the front door. His father was coming out of the kitchen to see who was doing all the shouting outside so late in the evening. Harsh voices out in the darkness of the street. Jimmy got out in the hallway ahead of his father and found himself between his pa and the knackered old door. Pa had a hurley in his hand, the stick held in front of him, as the soldier came crashing through the door. In the gloomy hall, the stick looked like a rifle.

Jimmy was only ten. The soldier looked huge to him. The man raised his real rifle and fired. The sound was deafening, Jimmy fell back away from the flash of the muzzle and saw his father stumble back too, like he'd been thumped in the chest.

The sound of the shot made Jimmy flinch and he snapped awake. It happened the same way every time. He always woke at the gunshot. Coughing a curse, he looked around him. He was leaning heavily against the wall of the mucky trench. With a groan, he shrugged at the straps digging into his shoulders, trying to shift his heavy kit into a more comfortable position.

Standing up straighter, he took off his helmet and rubbed a hand over his face and into his curly brown hair, which was damp with sweat. It was the 1st of July 1916, and the morning sun was already high enough over no-man's-land to relieve some of the gloom in the trench, but the air was murky with smoke. He checked his watch.

Quarter past seven. Fifteen minutes to go.

His hands trembled slightly. He slapped his deeply dimpled cheeks, then turned and picked up his rifle, which was leaning against one of the wooden supports reinforcing the earth wall.

'How in God's name can you fall asleep standin' up?' Seán exclaimed from beside him. 'And with all this racket?'

The air was filled with the thunder of the artillery smashing the German positions ahead of the 'Big Push'. Explosions thumped the earth like a giant's fists.

'It's a gift,' Jimmy replied, shifting his straps again. 'Besides, I didn't sleep last night.'

'Nobody slept last night, Jimmy. Sure, how could we?'

Seán McCabe was a freckled, thatch-headed young man with a horse-like face. He and Jimmy had been pals since before the war. They had grown up in the same area of Dublin.

Jimmy checked his watch. Fourteen minutes to go.

They were standing in a line of soldiers – a queue for one of the ladders that went up the front of the trench. They were waiting, frightened of what was to come, but hating the wait almost as much. The fear had left Jimmy exhausted, but restless and fidgety.

They both peered up the trench towards the captain, who was also glancing at his watch. Seán looked down at his Lee-Enfield rifle, working the bolt action over and over again, as he always did when he was nervous. It was the same model of gun that Jimmy held. Almost exactly the same type that had killed his father.

'I wonder about it sometimes,' Seán said, without looking up. 'You know, how you could wear the uniform after that. Seeing a British soldier kill your pa, I mean. Surprised you didn't join up with those rebels who caused all the trouble in Dublin at Easter.'

Jimmy turned his face away, remembering how his other friends had cursed him when he'd joined up to serve. How his mother had wept angry tears.

'Me dad wore the same uniform in his day, didn't he?' Jimmy retorted. 'He'd never have took up a gun against the government. Those soldiers came to the wrong house lookin' for some rebel who was holed up next door. Pa was shot by mistake, by an eejit. So I just...well, I thought soldierin' was a good job anyhow – better than a lot of things.'

'Oh, yeah,' Seán chuckled, slapping the bags of clay that lined the walls of their trench. 'This is a big step up, all right. And you get a far better class of rat in France. At least we had running water back in Dublin.'

They both looked around them. If you spent long enough in a trench, the dirt and the muck got everywhere. Everything ended up the same grey-brown colour after a while. And with no washing facilities and only crude latrines, the stink could knock out a dog.

Thirteen minutes to go.

Jimmy went over his kit again. It hung heavy on his shoulders, the ammunition pouches, bayonet, entrenching tool, water bottle, and other bits and pieces. He was hauling over sixty pounds, all told. Nearly half his own weight.

The men had been ordered to stand to, ready for the off. But having lined up by the ladders, there was nothing to do now but stand and wait. The terror was like a high-pitched sound they couldn't quite hear, but which shredded their nerves all the same.

Each man had his own way of coping with the

tension. Some smoked cigarettes, or whistled or sang softly, or repeatedly checked their kit, or their helmets, or their weapons.

Twelve minutes to go.

The two young men listened to the bombardment, the seemingly endless shelling of the German trenches. It had been going on for a week. The German positions were well fortified, but nothing could survive a pounding like that.

Jimmy and Seán were part of the 1st Battalion of the Royal Dublin Fusiliers – 'the Dubs' – one of the Irish regiments in the British Army. This company was among the last of the regular army to have served before the war. Most of the rest were dead.

They were experienced, professional soldiers, capable of the famous 'mad minute' – firing as many as thirty accurate shots with their rifles in the space of a minute. They had survived the disastrous first landing on the beaches of Gallipoli, where their battalion had been massacred by the machine guns of the Turkish defenders.

Eleven minutes to go.

Now they were here in France near the River Somme. They were stationed by the village of Beaumont-Hamel, looking out on a spot called Hawthorn Ridge.

Jimmy listened to the storm of artillery shells. It

was a hellish thing to be on the sharp end of a barrage. The noise was a crushing clamour that blotted out all thought. When the impacts got close, it felt like they were hammering your very skeleton. It put the horrors in you. Even if your bunker saved you from a direct hit, you might be buried alive in the process.

'They say they've fired a million shells at the Hun,' Jimmy said. 'A million. There must be nothing left over there.'

'I heard it's even more than that,' Seán sniffed. 'Even if you were still alive, dug in somewhere, how could you stand it? It'd drive a man out of his mind.'

The men had all become conditioned to the distant noise of the shelling. But the next sound was like something from another world.

Hawthorn Ridge exploded. The whole damn thing.

The ground wrenched violently beneath Jimmy's feet and he was almost knocked over. He looked up in shock to see hundreds of tons of earth, thousands, thrown into the sky. Planks of wood and loose bags of clay toppled from the trench wall. Men staggered, struggling to keep their balance, weighed down as they were with all their kit.

'It must be one of the mines,' Seán spluttered. 'Dear God in heaven!'

Jimmy nodded. Tunnels had been dug under some of the German positions to lay thousands of pounds of explosives right under the enemy's feet. The Dubs were stunned, their ears ringing from the sound of it. They gaped at the gigantic mushrooming cloud of soil, stones and smoke, for none of them had seen anything like it.

'It's plain bloody murder,' Jimmy said softly.

'What's that?' Seán asked.

'Look at that,' Jimmy rasped as the tons of debris fell to earth. There could be hundreds dead after that.'

'Aye, and good riddance!'

'It's not man against man in this war, Seán,' Jimmy said, his eyes looking black and hollowed out. 'It's industrial slaughter – sendin' men to be ground up like meat by bombs and machine guns.'

'Jaysus, Jimmy! Will you ever pipe down!' Seán urged him in a hoarse whisper. 'If the captain hears you, he'll have you tied to a gun wheel – or worse! He could have you shot for treason, for God's sake!'

At the mention of the captain, Jimmy saw the officer look at his watch, and he looked at his own. Twenty past seven. Surely they should charge now? If there were any Germans left, they'd still be in shock from the mine's explosion. They should go now. But the soldiers all knew they weren't going over the top until half past.

So they continued to wait. Just ten minutes, but it felt like hours.

'At least there'll be nobody left to fight,' Seán muttered. 'It should have cleared most of the Hun's barbed wire too. And the captain said the Hun's got no artillery behind those positions either.'

Five minutes to go.

Jimmy found himself thinking of his father again, and of the soldier who'd killed him. Seán was righter about that then he knew. Jimmy had hated the British for a long time. Still, you had to get on with life, didn't you? The Irish served in their army, and he was the youngest son in a poor family and had joined up underage because there was nothing better on offer. Now, he knew plenty of Brit lads and they were all right, mostly. But his father's death still haunted his dreams. Part of him thought he might yet find the man who'd shot his pa out here someday. And that he might kill the man if he did find him.

Three minutes.

The artillery barrage continued. The captain ordered his men to fix bayonets. Each man clicked the long knife into place on the end of his rifle. Once they reached the German trenches, the fighting would become all close-in and medieval in its brutality. But it was a job they had to do, so they would get on and do it.

One minute.

Jimmy's breathing and pulse quickened. His bladder felt too full. He was sweating so much, he had to grip his rifle tightly to stop it slipping in his hands.

This had once been a quiet area of fields and trees. The war had turned it into muddy carnage, pierced by shattered tree stumps, littered with bomb craters and strewn with stretches of barbed wire. Zigzagging trenches were filled with teeming armies of men, keeping their heads down, like parasites in the folds of the earth's skin.

The thought of it made Jimmy scratch at the itching caused by the lice in his armpits. All the men suffered from them. He remembered how his mother used to comb the children's hair for nits at bath-time. She was alone at home now.

He was struck with a sudden, seething hatred for the rebels who'd started all that violence back in Dublin while he was stuck out here. Sure, he wanted the British off the old sod too, but what those nationalists had done – trying to kick off a revolution in Ireland while Irish men were dying in their thousands over here in France and Belgium? That was a treacherous thing.

Half past seven. Time to go.

The captain checked his watch, paused for a moment, then took a breath and blew his whistle. Jimmy felt his heart pound like a hammer. One by one, the Dubs climbed out of the relative safety of the trench and stepped onto no-man's-land.

Then the German artillery opened up on them.

The guns the officers said weren't there.

And even as explosions began to burst the ground around them, machine guns let rip from the enemy positions, even from the crater left by the explosion on Hawthorn Ridge. Bullets zipped past like insanely fast insects. Hot metal shrapnel sprayed, designed to tear and pulverise flesh.

'Sweet Jesus!' Jimmy muttered.

There were Germans still alive, after all that pounding. Their bunkers had somehow kept them safe through a week of bombardment and now they were up and ready for it.

'Christ, we're going to get slaughtered!' Seán exclaimed, though Jimmy was barely able to hear him over the noise.

But there was a job to be done, and they had to get over there and do it. And so the Dubs formed a line across the devastated land, and began to advance through the smoke. Straight into an onslaught of artillery and machine-gun fire – from guns that weren't supposed to be there.

It was hard to keep the line together, carrying heavy kit across ploughed-up ground, clambering in and out of bomb craters. Men started to drop as the hurricane of bullets and bomb blasts did its damage. The screams began, the cries for help, but their friends were forbidden to stop.

They were barely past their own tangled, coiled rows of barbed wire, when Jimmy looked to his right to see how Seán was doing. Just at that moment, something like a brick wall slammed into him from the left, hitting him with a noise that felt like it would crush his skull. The ground heaved up and thumped into him from the right and seemed to swallow him, sounds becoming distant and muffled.

And then there was nothing.

Jimmy could feel pain in his arm like it was still there. Phantom pain, the nurse had called it. His body wanted his arm to still be there. But every time he looked down, there it was...gone. Like picking at a scab, he couldn't bear the sight of the bandaged stump halfway down his upper left arm – and yet he kept looking at it.

His thoughts were muddled all the time. The constant ringing in his ears didn't help. He'd woken up three days ago. He'd been lucky. Seán was in a bad state too, with shrapnel in his face and all down his left side, after that shell exploded next to them. But he'd saved Jimmy's life by getting a tourniquet on the mess that was his arm.

They were both injured close to their own front lines, early in the battle, so the lads from the Royal Army Medical Corps were able to rush them back to the Casualty Clearing Station, the temporary hospital in Amiens. Jimmy and Seán's wounds were patched up, and Jimmy's ruined arm was amputated.

'Will you look at that,' Seán said.

Jimmy nodded. Yet another horde of casualties in khaki was arriving at the tents. Those who could walk had to get to the hospital under their own steam. Others were on stretchers. They were all caked in blood and sweat and mud.

The hospital was overwhelmed, a crowded slum of damaged bodies. The surgeons and nurses were worked to the point of exhaustion. The Big Push was turning into the worst disaster in the history of the British Army. Most of the lads from Jimmy's company were dead, along with thousands of others.

Jimmy and Seán were among a group of men who had been moved out of the evacuation tent, and were now sitting on a grassy bank looking out on the railway line. They were waiting for the train to take them to the coast, where they would be transferred onto one of the hospital ships. The men huddled with blankets around them, some of them babbling or shaking, others staring into nothingness, not uttering a word. Everyone wore bloodstained bandages.

There were newspapers being handed around. Seán was reading in one of them about the aftermath of the Easter Rising by the group who called themselves 'the Irish Volunteers'.

'They've executed all the leaders of the rebellion back home,' he told Jimmy. 'Sixteen of them. Pearse, Clarke…Connolly too. Firing squad for the lot of 'em.'

'James Connolly? I thought he'd been taken injured?' Jimmy said.

'He was. They tied him to a chair to keep him upright as they shot him.'

About two months earlier, at Easter, nationalist rebels had taken advantage of the war in Europe. In an attempt to drive the British out of Ireland, they took over key areas of Dublin and a few other locations around the country and declared an independent republic. They came in uniform, armed with pistols and rifles, and had held on for the best part of a week as the British Army tried to dig them out. Three battalions of Jimmy and Seán's regiment, the Royal Dublin Fusiliers, had been among the soldiers who did battle with the rebels. Irishmen killing Irishmen.

The so-called 'Volunteers' didn't receive the support they'd hoped for from the Irish people, but they still proved to be a serious threat. In the end, the British forces had resorted to artillery, including sailing gunboats up the Liffey. Whole areas of Dublin had been bombarded like they were trenches in the war. More than four hundred people died in the fighting – over two hundred of them civilians. Most of them were killed by artillery.

Now the men who'd led the rebellion had been shot as traitors to Britain, and despite all the death Jimmy had seen here, those sixteen executions had unsettled him.

'It was murder, pure and simple,' said another man, named Butler, who was sitting with them.

He was a Kilkenny man, small with a wiry build and light brown hair that was encrusted with blood. A bandage wrapped around his head covered a bad scalp wound.

'The ordinary people had no appetite for violent revolution,' the man said. 'But the executions will change things. This'll get people's backs up.'

'Those men were traitors,' Seán growled, a grimace on his bandaged face at the pain in his injured side. 'They got what they deserved.'

'We don't execute German prisoners, do we?' Butler retorted. 'But it's all right to shoot the Irish?'

'That must have been a bad knock on the head you took,' Seán snapped. 'The Germans are fighting for their country, we're fighting for ours. Connolly and those others betrayed their country.'

'Ireland *is* their country,' Butler said sharply. 'Not Britain. Not Britain! The men – and women – who took over Dublin swore loyalty to an Irish state. They fought in uniform, under an Irish flag. They see Britain the way the British see Germany. When those men were captured, they were prisoners of war, not traitors.'

'That's treasonous talk, right there,' Seán hissed.

'That may be,' Butler said, taking a crutch and getting to his feet. 'But I'll tell you now, I'll be a dog for the British generals no longer. There's only two choices for an Irishman now. Either the Brits give Ireland its own parliament, or we kick them out altogether, and take the whole damn country back.'

Leaning on his crutch, the man hobbled off.

Jimmy watched him go, struggling to make sense of his thoughts. On a road nearby, he saw several sixty-pounder guns being pulled towards the front line by shire horses. He shivered as he looked at them. He was amazed that the generals were still pushing on with this attack along the Somme after so many men had died.

'It's a murder machine,' he said again.

'What's that, Jimmy?' Seán asked.

'See what they've done to us,' Jimmy rasped, gesturing at the scene before them. 'There's toffs takin' sugar cubes in their tea, miles behind the lines, while they order us off into the jaws of that… that…that German killing factory over yonder. And the German officers send their men to the same over here. That's not fightin' – it's mass murder.'

'Mind what you say,' Seán cautioned him. 'You're startin' to sound like one of them rebels.'

'At least their leaders stood with them,' Jimmy replied. 'They believed enough in what they were doing to die for it. I don't agree with what they did, but they had a kind of honour about them, Seán.'

'They were shooting soldiers in Dublin on the same day there were Irish lads over here, gettin' blinded by poison gas in Hulluch, Jimmy,' Seán snarled. 'Getting their lungs burned out. That's honour, is it?'

'That's a different thing,' Jimmy said, shaking his head and wincing at the pain of it. 'What about the troops firin' artillery into Dublin? Look at the state of us two, Seán. This thing that's happened to you and me – those guns tore up people sitting in their own *homes* in Dublin. Fightin's a dirty business whatever way you look at it, but with war, it's like death gets so huge and hungry, it starts thunderin' along by itself, with nobody even stokin' the fires any more.'

'What are you saying, Jimmy?' Seán asked in a cold voice.

The left half of his face, including his eye, was covered in bandages. His left arm was in a sling, his right eye was badly bloodshot and his nostrils were rimmed with blood. He was not happy about this talk, and he had a fearsome expression on his face.

'I'm sayin'...aw, I don't know, Seán,' Jimmy groaned. 'This stuff is beyond me. Maybe it's that someone has to decide not to kill someone else sometimes, I suppose. So it doesn't just keeping goin' on. Like those rebel leaders. Maybe they shouldn't have been shot, that's all.'

'You think what you like, Jimmy. But they tried to take over the country,' Seán said, his unbandaged eye wide with hostility. 'And I'd never hand Ireland over to those traitors. I'd trust them no further than I'd trust the lice in my crotch. You stick that in your pipe and smoke it, Jimmy Reilly, while you're doin' your ponderin'.'

Jimmy didn't reply, already beginning to understand that he and his friend would never see eye to eye on this. In fact, they said little at all to each other after that, on the long and painful journey home.

Jimmy lost touch with Seán after they returned to Ireland. They were both bitter and angry when they returned, but for very different reasons. The country had changed a great deal, and nor was it done changing. Four years passed before the two friends looked set to meet again.

Jimmy scratched the base of his stump as he lay on his side in the long damp grass. The empty sleeve of his jacket was pinned up in a fold, and it was hard to get at the itch through the thick material. He peered through the bramble hedge at the two-storey stone building with the slate roof that stood on the far side of the road. His Webley revolver lay in the grass in front of him.

He was reminded of that first day of the Somme. His last day in the trenches. It was a morning like this; early, with the sun already quite high, but the hill behind the building was still in shadow. Taking his watch out and looking at it, Jimmy thought of his captain that day as they waited to go over the top.

'Tommy says your mate's in there,' Mick said to him. 'The one from the war.'

'He's not my mate,' Jimmy answered. 'So don't go treating him like one.'

'What, you mean you don't want us to be all polite, like? And here I thought we were giving the Tans time to let their breakfast settle.'

'We are, right enough,' Jimmy replied, grinning. 'The best time to get a man to surrender is halfway through his cup o' tea.'

Jimmy glanced either side of him, and at the bushes up the hill behind the police barracks, to check his men were in position. Mick Rogan, his second-in-command, lay beside him. The Meath man had a Lee-Enfield in his hands. The same type of gun a British soldier had used to kill Jimmy's father. The same type Jimmy had used in the war. A lot of those rifles had found their way into the hands of rebels when Irish soldiers came home from the front to find their country in a crisis, with rebel forces fighting for independence from the British.

Those soldiers came home to find their country in a crisis that was gradually building into another conflict. It was one that might be less destructive, but was all the more bitter. Government buildings, soldiers, intelligence officers and even policemen were targeted by the rebels. And even though this war was being waged against the British, many of the men who served Britain were Irish.

The rebels had learned their lesson from the Easter Rising. They didn't have the numbers or weapons to beat the overwhelming force of the British Army in a conventional battle. Most of their attacks were waged by small flying columns of guerrilla fighters who struck suddenly and then disappeared. People were starting to call it the War of Independence.

Jimmy had got involved in campaigning against Irish involvement in the war over in France and Belgium, but he had initially steered clear of the men who preached violence against the British, who wanted him to put his fighting skills to good use. The turning point for him came, however, in early 1918 when the British government tried to introduce conscription in Ireland.

Jimmy was enraged by the move. He would not stand by as British politicians tried to force Irishmen to march off and die in the trenches. He joined the rebel forces, along with many like him. His military experience made him valuable to the cause and he quickly proved himself to be a cunning leader, and was given command of his own squad.

Now the year was 1920 and Jimmy lay in a field behind a hedge in County Cork. He was there with a squad of armed rebels, looking out at a police barracks. And one of the men inside that square stone block of a place was Seán McCabe, now a sergeant in the Royal Irish Constabulary.

'Tommy reckons there's at least six Black and Tans in there,' Mick told him. 'If we don't get them out, this could all go arseways.'

'We'll just have to put the fear of God into them then, won't we?' Jimmy answered.

Black and Tans were former soldiers, recruited to reinforce the RIC, but given little police training. These 'temporary constables' were notorious for killing civilians and destroying property, and represented everything that was most hated about British rule in Ireland.

But it was their weapons Jimmy wanted. The barracks had an armoury of rifles, pistols and thousands of rounds of ammunition. A valuable haul for a guerrilla army with few supplies of their own.

'All right, let's do it,' he said.

The building was big for a house, but small for a barracks. Tommy, the squad's best scout approached from the side, leading two other men down the hill, out of sight of the windows. Each man took position under a window at the front.

Jimmy signalled with his hand. Each of the three rebels pulled the pin from a Mills bomb, smashed a pane in the window above them and tossed the smoking grenade in. Then they fired a few loose shots through the windows to make sure those inside didn't try and throw the bombs back out again.

Moments later, the front door was flung open and about ten men in RIC and Black and Tan uniforms came rushing out in a panic. Jimmy and six others were outside waiting for them, guns at the ready. The escaping men turned, hands up covering their heads, no doubt expecting to see explosions blowing out the windows.

There were no explosions. The grenades were rigged – they had fuses, but no explosives in them. Jimmy didn't want a massacre – he just wanted the building cleared in a hurry, and with as few casualties as possible. And he wanted the armoury intact.

Seán was one of the men in uniform. He spotted Jimmy and a sour scowl twisted his face.

'Jimmy bloody Reilly!' he snarled.

'Howaya, Seán,' Jimmy greeted him brightly. 'We'll be takin' your guns, if you don't mind!'

As the other lads began tying up the policemen, Jimmy, Mick and a couple of others ran straight past them and into the building.

They had to be careful of stragglers, the odd one or two who might still be left in the building. Jimmy had his pistol raised as he moved from room to room. He came to a closed door and kicked it open. A storeroom, well-stocked, but empty of people. He was just turning when someone stepped out of the doorway behind him and to his left. There was only an instant to react, and Jimmy had no left arm to fend off the blow that might be coming. Jimmy saw the flash of a hand being lifted and he turned and fired point-blank into the man's chest.

The gunshot was loud in the small hallway, resounding off the solid walls. The stink of cordite filled Jimmy's nostrils even as he watched the man topple away from him, the bullet-hole a few inches above his heart.

The man, dressed in civilian clothes, collapsed against the doorframe. From the room beyond, Jimmy saw a boy no older than ten or eleven rush to the man as he fell.

'Pa! Pa!' the boy shouted, terror in his voice, wrapping his arms around his father's neck.

Jimmy stared in consternation. Why was there a child here, in a barracks? He stood gaping at the boy, his smoking revolver dangling from limp fingers. The boy tried to put his hand over the hole in the man's chest, and Jimmy felt a sudden urge to throw up as he saw the blood well up between the child's fingers.

'Jim! Jimmy!' Mick yelled from down the hallway. 'The guns are down here! Jimmy, what's up with you?'

Jimmy was transfixed by the injured man's face.

At first he thought it was him – the soldier who'd killed Jimmy's father. Right here right now, bleeding at Jimmy's feet. But it was just a passing resemblance, Jimmy's mind grasping at the hope that this was a righteous shooting. No, this was a young man in farmer's clothes, a form clutched in his clenched hand; just some local man, here with his son to conduct some business, or perhaps just to ask one of the better educated policemen to help with reading that form.

The boy glared up at Jimmy with a mixture of horror and pure hatred. And Jimmy understood exactly what he was feeling.

Mick came up the hallway towards him, his rifle held warily before him.

'Come on, man!' he said. 'Jimmy, wake up! Let's get this place cleared out, for God's sake!'

Tucking his revolver into his belt, Jimmy took out his handkerchief, crouched down by the wounded man and gently pushed the boy's hands away. He folded up the square of linen and pressed it hard against the bloody hole.

'Find the medical supplies,' he said to Mick.

'We haven't time for this!' Mick protested. 'There could be more Tans on their way back here any minute.'

'Then take the bloody guns and go!' Jimmy

replied in a choked voice. He cleared his throat and said more clearly: 'You take them – sort the lads out. Look after them. I'm stayin' here.'

Mick grimaced and disappeared down the hall, returning a minute later with a box of bandages. He dropped it on the floor, looking over Jimmy's shoulder at the boy.

'It's an ugly business, all right,' he said. 'But we can't hang about. We need to go, Jim.'

Jimmy tore open the box and began dressing the man's wound. The boy's father had a savage look on his face. He was spitting blood, drops of stark red on skin that was white as paper. But Jimmy thought he might be all right if the flow of blood could be stemmed until a doctor could get here. The bullet hadn't found the heart. The man had a chance.

'Go on, Mick.'

'You could be caught, Jimmy!'

'Ah, don't be such a bleatin' old woman! I can take care of myself. Now go!'

He finished bandaging the wound as the lads began carrying out the guns and boxes of ammunition behind him. Sitting down on the floor, he gazed into the faces of the father and son. One eyed him weakly; wary, but scared of dying. The other had a look of barely contained terror, held in check by something more intense and lasting.

Jimmy met the boy's eyes. There was nothing he could say to that lad that would mean anything, but Jimmy knew right then he was done killing. He took the revolver from his belt and laid it down on the floor beside him, pointing it away from the man and his son.

'I thought this was the only way we could win out,' he said to them, gesturing towards the gun, as if it was every kind of gun. He wasn't sure if he meant it as an apology or not. 'But it's like death gets so hungry, it starts thunderin' along by itself.'

He looked at them for another minute, and they looked back at him.

'I'll send a doctor to you,' he said.

He felt he should say so much more, but he knew that bullet wound would make all his words meaningless to them. Bullet wounds had that effect on people.

'So that's it, then,' he added finally.

And he got up and walked out, leaving them and his gun there on the cold floor of the barracks hallway.

FIREWORKS
Geraldine McCaughrean

Author's note:

*The Great War isn't simply a gaping wound in history.
It bled over its edges into peacetime, as all wars do. Many
men never spoke about their time at the Front. Either they
wanted to protect their families from seeing it 'second-hand';
or the horrors were simply beyond words; or they hoped to
bury the memories so deep none could ever crawl out of
the mud to haunt them. But because men had been made to
bear the unbearable, hundreds of thousands came home
maimed in ways that didn't show on the outside. They are
the ones I chose to write about.*

There were a lot of homecoming parties. They were happening all over town. Some people said it was hard on anyone whose men weren't coming home. But when your dad's a hero, you want to make a song and dance about it, don't you? So I was all in favour of the street holding a party. Anyway, there were the fireworks.

Years old, they were. I found them in the loft. Ma said Dad bought them ready for Bonfire Night in 1914, but then he enlisted and was gone by November the Fifth, and she hadn't felt like celebrating. Fair-do's, I suppose. Dad bought them. It's only right he should be there to set them off.

No one else on the street was going to have fireworks; none in the shops any more – no makings, or something. But we'd have them. Rich was scummy about it. He said that I 'always got the luck'.

We used to be mates, but he went really rum after his Dad came home, two years back. 'Invalided out', that's how Rich explained it. Right.

I told Rich, I told him: 'Why's he an invalid? I can't see anything much wrong with him,' and he punched me. End of a lovely friendship, know what I mean? He was jealous, I reckon, because his father's only a corporal and a shirker, and mine's a full captain and a hero with a medal to prove it.

Ma said no to the fireworks. She said it might be – how's this? – 'a bit noisy'. Noisy? Blimey! They were ringing the church bells for twelve hours the day the war ended. You couldn't hear yourself think.

It's all right, though. I can get round Ma. During the war we found out: you can do all kinds of things when there are no men around to make you wish you hadn't. No real men. Just the Old Codgers. The best way with mothers, though, is not to tell them things. Then if a scheme goes well, you say it was a Surprise. If it goes badly, you say it was Someone Else's Idea. So I didn't tell Ma about my plans for the Grand Firework Display. Nobody's going to mind a bit of noise in a good cause.

I told my mates, though – and Rich – because I wanted them to know our house would be having the best party. There's nothing like scoring over your friends.

'It's not a competition,' said Rich. Where's he been living all these years? Of course it is.

We're deeply competitive down our street. Ma is out there every morning, scrubbing the front doorstep. I bet that, once, our step was square and sharp-edged, like with the staircase inside, but she's scrubbed it so often that she's worn it down to cushion-shaped and roundy. All the women do it round here. With Dad coming home, she outdid them all. She *painted* it. Little tin of cardinal red paint from the ironmongers, a paintbrush stiff as a fork, from the drawer in the shed. Now the step gleams like a slab of fresh liver.

When Dad came home, he noticed it straightaway. He wouldn't step on it even, for fear of spoiling it. (Or he might have thought the paint was still wet.)

It was odd seeing him: I thought I remembered exactly how he looked. We said goodnight to the photograph on the sideboard, all the time he was away. But when he got here, I hardly recognised him. He was big with greatcoat, but his face looked so much thinner than in the photograph on the sideboard – thin, and scored with lines, like someone's taken a penknife to him. It was all hugs and tears and presents, of course, and Ma cooking him all his favourite meals. (We haven't eaten that well all the time he's been gone.) But it's still strange, having him in the house. I don't know why, but I'm kind of nervous of him.

When I try to tell him things about cricket or school or new people on the street, it's like he's trying to listen to something else, and I'm making it harder by talking. He looks as if he'd rather know what's happening in the next room – or what they're saying next door. Sometimes he looks at me and his eyes aren't *looking*. Know what I mean? It's like they're switched off. Every day I ask him to tell us about his Heroic Exploits. I want to know. I *need* to know; Ned and Jonno are after me to tell them. But every time I ask, Dad just makes a face like he's going to sneeze, or he gives a snort like a pig, and won't tell any of us a thing.

It's *sang froid*. I read about it. It's very English (though I don't know why you'd have a French word for something that's very English). It means 'cold blood'. I thought that was what lizards and snakes have, but apparently *sang froid* means more 'cool and collected in a crisis'. Heroes have it in spades. Cowards don't. Rich's dad doesn't have *sang froid*: he's just Corporal Cold Fish.

Of course anything Ma and I say must be boring in comparison with what they talked about in the trenches: guns and shells and missions behind enemy lines... Dad probably misses the excitement, and people saluting him. That's why I'm glad I've got the fireworks in reserve. That'll show him life's not going to be dull *every* day now he's home.

I asked Miss Bone if she wanted Dad to come into school and talk to the class about being a hero, but she said it would be hard for children who've lost someone: 'A brother or a father or an uncle or a grandfather. Or a sweetheart.' Crikey, how we laughed about that. She's always an odd bod, Miss Bone, but some girl in Top Juniors having a sweetheart dead in the war? I don't think so.

Maybe Dad will open up at the party – when there's beer and sherry and cucumber sandwiches – and tell us how he got his medal and a captain's commission.

On the other side of the street, opposite our houses, a train runs along the top of an embankment. (What with all the demobbed soldiers travelling home, there have been dozens of extra trains lately.) I'm setting the fireworks up on the embankment. Even in broad daylight no one will notice me, because all the women are in their kitchens, cooking for the party. If I had a piece of fuse, I could link all the fireworks up to each other. Then I wouldn't need to be on the hill to light them. I could just light one and then run down and stand beside Dad in the front garden and get the full effect: hear what he has to say about it.

But at least from up on the embankment I'll be able to see how my Big Surprise goes down; see all the faces light up, green and blue and red and impressed. I've put the rockets in milk bottles – (yes, pointing away from the houses: I'm not stupid).

These are top-hole fireworks. Even before the war they must have cost a fortune.

What I really want is to end up with a big V for Victory, like in the firework display they did on the headland to 'bid the boys farewell'. I don't remember much of that. Apparently I got scared by the bangs and hid my face in Ma's skirt, and wouldn't look till right at the end, so I only saw the V. That I remember. It was like those brands cowboys put on horses in cowboy books, except it was burned into the sky. I was only six or seven or something, but what a stupid waste of a fireworks display that was, hiding my face in Ma's skirt. Little kids are stupid about bangs.

I'll make up for it in a couple of hours. There are plenty of bangers in the box. Rick-racks and the like. It's going to be tickety-binky-boo, my Grand Display. I've even thought of a way of doing the Victory V.

'It's not a victory,' says Rich, and he's standing there, watching me get grass stains on my knees as I lay out my big secret. He could spoil everything, so I can't tell him he's a barmpot.

'We won, didn't we?'

'Did we?' he asks. 'Say you go to the fair and you get three hoops over three skittles. And what do they give you? A bucket of brains, your best friend's leg, a bottle of phosgene gas, and lice. Then they stick your dog with a bayonet. Would you feel like a winner? Ask your dad.'

'What d'you know? You don't know anything about it.'

'Broke everything. Killed everyone. Sent home the empties. That's about the sum of it.'

That's his father talking. He doesn't know anything about it. Rich wasn't there, any more than I was. But he's going to spoil everything if he goes and tells about the fireworks. So I say:

'You want to help me set these out?'

It takes ages. By the time we're finishing, we can smell the sausages cooking. Ma has made punch and egg-and-bacon flan. There's luncheon meat and tongue and drop-scones and some black-pudding. I don't know where the beer came from, but there's a *lot* of beer being drunk. I'll ask Dad for a sip of his later, after The Surprise. Some of the women have started to sing – 'There's No Place Like Home' and 'Danny Boy' – at the same time, at opposite ends of the street. (I said we were competitive down our way.) By the time Rich and I are setting off down the embankment, the parties have bled out of the houses and into the street. Most of the boys from school are sauntering down towards our end, because they know about the fireworks. But I won't set anything off until eight o'clock. Deep dark is best. I'm pretty happy that Rich stayed on and helped...even if he is a maundering wet echo.

Dad's laughing and the neighbours are all flirting with him, because his hair's growing back and he's got his captain's uniform on and he looks like 'Hounslow Heath the Highwayman' in *Chips* comics. He's got a swagger to him, and I want to say to Rich, 'Look at that. That's a real dad. That's what a hero looks like, in case you've never seen one.' But Rich has started back down, and I follow him, lured by sausages.

Then the six-thirty train goes by, braking late like it always does, spraying its little plume of golden sparks from under the wheels.

And I suppose one of the sparks found the rick-racks, because all of a sudden there's a terrific rattle of bangs right behind us.

Me, I'm stood on one foot, wondering where to put the other one. Do I run back up the slope to try and stop the rick-racks setting light to anything else? Or do I pretend it's all part of the plan? I'm still thinking about it when the first rocket goes off, its blue touch paper lit by the grass (which has nicely caught fire now). Forty faces turn towards the sky, and there's my dad's face among them. It's like his skull is showing through his skin. I can see his teeth and his jaw bone, and his mouth's a great hole in the middle – a giant silent scream.

First his knees go, and then he's crawling along the ground, and he's got one hand over the back of his head. The Old Codgers don't see, because they're all running towards me – towards the embankment, to try and put out the grass fire.

But Dad isn't.

He's grovelling on the floor, swearing and screaming and sobbing, and the women are standing with their cucumber sandwiches halfway to their mouths, looking at him. Even Ma doesn't know what to do, except squat down and shout his name at him. 'Eric. Eric? Eric! Eric, don't. Eric, stop it this instant.'

My mates are sort of backing away. They're torn between watching the rockets going off in all directions as the milk bottles topple, and watching my dad try to climb into the coal hole. He won't manage it – the handle's come off the lid a year back and he wasn't here to mend it. He's gibbering and juddering, like he's cold to the marrow.

The fireworks are all going off at once, as the fire crawls down the embankment. There are puddling piddling springs of green light, like rupturing boils, and sparks from the sparklers I was going to use to write 'WELCOME HOME DAD' in the air. Some are just exploding with nothing to show for it but noise – and the look on Dad's face.

Every bang drags his lips farther back off his teeth. His nose is running – I can see it perfectly clearly by the light from the hall window. There's a noise coming out of him too, like a baby choking to death in its cot. And when he can't get into the coal hole, he crawls down the slot beside it where we prop up the yard broom and spade and hoe and clothes horse, so that they all clatter round about him and tumble onto the path. Now my mates are looking from him to me and me to him, and their mouths are half grinning because of the mayhem going on, and they're half crouched for fear of rocket injury, so they look like trolls or something. I hate them all.

Ma's staring at the troll down the slot beside the coal bunker. I'm thinking *Get him out. Get him out, why don't you? Make him stop. Get him out of sight.*

Why don't I do it for her? Because if I go near him I'll be admitting he's something to do with me, and I don't want to be anything to do with that loony man.

It's Rich's dad who comes. It feels like hours, but it's not two minutes before Rich's dad comes running. He must have been heading for the embankment, because he's carrying an empty coal sack for swatting the fire. But when he sees the circus going on in our garden, he takes it all in, lightning fast. He vaults over the garden wall, straight into the heart of the whole terrible shemozzle. Then he shoos everyone away with the sack, like they're flies round meat.

'Right away. Right away,' he tells them, and they believe him instantly because of the way he says it. Even Ma moves back against the fence.

And Corporal Cold Fish sprawls across the coal bunker, and reaches over the side, and sort of levers Dad to his feet, telling him, 'We'll go inside now, shall we, sir? Let's go inside now, sir.'

Then they get to the doorstep, the newly painted step, all shiny cardinal red in the hall light, and Dad lurches backwards, saying he won't tread on it.

'I won't tread on him! I won't tread on any more. Who is it? Who is it? Is he ours or theirs?' And he steps back and trips on the hoe and sits down hard, still trying to pull away from the cardinal-red doorstep.

Corporal Cold Fish takes hold of Dad like a baby and rocks him in his arms, and looks him in the face – full in the eyes, their faces so close the tips of their noses brush. 'It's all right, sir. It's all right, sir. It's just a horse. It's not a man, it's just a horse. Look at me, not the horse, sir. Look at me. Can you hear me? It's not our turn, sir. It's just the Welsh getting it tonight. Just the Taffs. You know what you should do, sir? You should get some shut-eye. Relief column'll be here in the morning. We're stepped down tomorrow, sir. Remember? They're stepping us down tomorrow.' And he gets the sack and holds it up, so that Dad can't see the step – red as fresh liver – can't see the grass fire or the gawping faces.

The last of the milk bottles on the hill tips over and starts to roll diagonally down the hill. It comes right by me, so close that I can see the rocket's cane rolling round in the neck of the bottle. Then with no more than a *phutt*, it takes off for the house.

It just misses the beer tankard balanced on the garden wall, but it doesn't miss Rich's dad. It hits him full in the back. I catch my breath so sharply that I start coughing and I can't stop. It must have hurt like hell, but he doesn't jump up yelling and wanting to kill me. He doesn't move a muscle. He just folds himself over Dad to shield him better, and he goes on rocking him, rocking him, and talking to him and telling him how they'll be going down the line tomorrow for some R and R. Rest and recreation.

What with all the smoke and the stink of cordite, I can't stop coughing now I've started. Coughing and coughing. Something like coughing, anyway.

Rich puts a hand on my back.

FIREWORKS

'He's still there,' he says. 'Your dad. He's still over there. He hasn't left the war behind yet – can't get it out of his head. Mine was the same for a year. He came home, but his head was still in Belgium, still in Mons. He dreamed it every night. I could hear him through the wall. Anything loud – a truck going over the cattle grid; anything sudden – a hare in the field – and he was back there. Mud and blood, blood and mud and terror: that's all it was, he said. It gets better. He's getting better, look. He'll be all right one day. So will yours.'

The old men are edging us both off the embankment now, working in a line, slapping at the grass fire, reducing it to a grey, smoking line. Their sacks and blankets scatter the burned-out remains of the fireworks and all the other litter people throw out of train windows.

'I suppose your dad saved some poor blighter, did he?' says Rich. 'To get his medal? Good man. Top hole. Now it's his turn to be the poor blighter, that's all. He just needs rescuing.'

Behind us, the patch of ground where I sprinkled the contents of a Roman candle to make a Victory V is spitting and hissing: I didn't have enough powder to make it any thicker than a snake. Pathetic. No one will even see it. But I'll always see it. Every time I go out the front door, I'll see where I branded that V into the flank of the hill – that two-finger sign – telling the world my dad was a hero...

...when that snivelling heap down there is all he is.

THE OTHER ANZAC DAY
Sophie Masson

Author's note:

*This story was inspired by the small town of
Villers-Bretonneux, near Amiens, in the Somme region
of northern France. It is where Australian regiments
won a decisive battle on Anzac Day 1918 (the 25th of April),
which even back then was known as 'the other Anzac Day',
(the first, in 1916, commemorated the Gallipoli landings
on April 25th 1915). As a French Australian, it has
an added poignancy for me – Anzac Day is celebrated
there every year.*

In single file we move silent as snakes through the wood, slipping down the sunken roads to take our positions. All is quiet. The machine guns are silent, thank Christ. Fritz is sleeping. We hope. The Poms are somewhere out there moving towards the town, and on the other side of us somewhere is the second Aussie brigade. It's a pincer movement, Owl had said. He's our resident professor. Reads all about military strategy for fun, draws little diagrams for us. See, here, he told me, that's how it'll be done, Archie, the Aussie battalions from the left and right, the Poms in the middle, no artillery attack first, right, just our weapons in hand, rifles and bayonets for most of us, machine guns for the gunners, total surprise. We knock out the machine gun nests, and we fall on Fritz before they even know we're there. Like tigers in ambush, like wolves on the fold, says Pat, who's something of a poet. Mate, says Snowy, snorting, them Boche aren't what you'd call meek little lambs, they fight like demons and don't you forget it.

There was a moon, but the clouds have swallowed it up now. There's a strange red light in the sky over the little town just past the wood and a smell that reminds me of last year when I was fighting that fire at the neighbour's back home. Houses are burning in the town, shelling's been going on for days and Villers-Bretonneux is rubble and burning houses and smoking ruins now. But one French bloke we spoke to the other day, an old farmer who's hung on and on like a tough tick on a cow, he told us that once the town was pretty and brisk as you please, a magnet for the little villages and farms around it, at least that's what Owl said he said, and as he's the only one of us who speaks proper Frog we got to trust him in that, hey?

The town might be flattened but the fields around are full of grass and flowers growing over the deep scars of old trenches all over. There was a lot of trench fighting in this district before, like in all of this Somme region, but now that's over. No animals, of course, right now but a few small crops starting to be planted. Looks like nice fertile country, you could get a mighty good yield here, my uncle back home would say.

It's a different kind of war to before, no more trenches. In the past it was mud and trenches from end to end of the Somme. Men lived in trenches, died in them. Now it's skirmishes and battles in woods and towns, more the sort like at the beginning of the war, Owl says. He says it's changed again now 'cos there's not so much a stalemate as before. The Yanks came in our side last year but there's not enough of 'em yet and now Jerry's got the advantage. They're stronger than for a long time. They've got lots of fresh new troops pouring in from the Eastern Front where the Russkies gave up fighting last year, and they've been launching lightning attacks all up and down the north of France and Belgium, pushing the Poms and the Frogs and us Colonials – Aussies and Canadians and New Zealanders – back and back.

That's why we're here, 'cos earlier this month Fritz took VB again, and though it's just a small town, it's important. You have VB, you have a direct shelling line to the city of Amiens from the hill near here. Hill 104, they call it, and then there's a Roman road straight as an arrow just right for an army to march right to the heart of that city once the way's cleared. And from Amiens, well, you are not that far to Paris.

It's important not to lose Amiens. It's important not to lose VB, no matter what, whatever it costs. And it's cost plenty. The Poms took heavy heavy losses two weeks ago. Hundreds of the poor beggars killed and injured. That might happen to us today but you can't think of that. You got to think, we got to take it back from Fritz. From Jerry. The Boche.

Whatever you want to call them out there in the darkness, the Germans, dug into the town and the surrounding woods and countryside. They're somewhere in here, with us. We got to find them before they find us…

My hand tightens on my weapon. I'm ready for them. I'm more than ready…

Hey boys, it's gone midnight, whispers Snowy. It's the 25th now. Anzac Day.

Good omen, I reckon, says Blue, and everyone nods.

Lest we forget, says Pat, and he says another few words, solemn-like, and for once no one tells him to shut his trap. But forget? Not a chance. We're all thinking of that very first Anzac Day. A surprise night attack, like this one. Gallipoli. The landing at the place we now call Anzac Cove. Three years to the day. Almost to the hour.

I remember the headlines in the newspapers the next day: *Glorious Deeds! Unsurpassed Daring of the Anzacs! Miracle of Bravery!* The day the Australian and New Zealand Army Corps really showed what we were capable of. When we wrote our new nations proudly into the roll call of glory. Australia and New Zealand's baptism of fire, a day to remember for ever.

I devoured every word. I was so proud. My older

brother Jamie was in one of the Anzac battalions there. Now, as we waited in ambush ourselves, I could just picture him as I remembered the reports about how after being given a good hot meal and a drink on board their ships the Anzacs had landed on that beach in the dead of night – a clear bright moonlit night, though, not like this one. Everyone was calm, ran the reports. Everyone was itching for battle but calm as you like. There were only whispers among the men, quiet footfalls, no loud noises. The Turks up on the heights were not expecting it. They were taken by surprise as up and down the coast the Allied forces – the French, the British, including the Anzacs – moved in by sea at night. But they recovered and the landing was soon raked by rifle and machine-gun fire from the cliffs. In some of the landing places the cliffs could be scaled more easily but at Anzac Cove the cliffs were so sheer, so steep that it proved almost impossible. Heavy casualties, reported the correspondents gravely, and there will be grief in many households, but such feats of incredible courage against great odds will give comfort.

I wish that had been true for my mother, I think, grasping my rifle. Yet when she got the telegram that Jamie would not be coming home, that he had been killed at faraway Gallipoli, she did not cry. Did not scream, like the mother of Norm Penny, up the road. Her screams, you could hear up and down the street. My mother said nothing. Sat in the chair with the telegram in her lap, staring into space. She sat like that for hours. Wouldn't talk. Wouldn't eat. Wouldn't even take a cup of tea, she who lived on tea from morning till night. Strewth, I didn't know what to do, so I went and fetched our next-door neighbour Mrs Hunt, who was good friends with Mum and who I thought might help. And she did, while sending me outside to chop up some firewood – you need to do something, love, she said, you're all jumpy and you're making it worse for her.

As I chopped and chopped, more wood than we'd use for weeks probably, though I was sweating from the effort, I could feel inside my throat something that sat like a hard cold lump. I knew what it was. I'd never see Jamie again. Never hear his laughing voice joshing me. Never have to put up with his calling me Kid Arch. Or Little Archie. Or Mini Bell. Six years older than me he was, and man of the house since Dad died when I was three. When I was real little I used to follow him around. Even after I stopped being his faithful dog, I liked being around him. He was a real good fella, though he could be blanky irritating with those nicknames.

I would miss him, I knew that. I'd miss him so bad. But I was also so proud of him. So proud. My brother. My only brother. He was a real honest-to-God hero. A hero of Anzac Cove.

I tried to say that to Mum, later. Much later. Maybe it was the wrong thing to say. Women don't see things the way we do. I wasn't trying to say that it didn't matter Jamie was gone. It mattered terribly. There would always be that empty place in me that was the ache for him. But it made it better, to know he'd died a hero. When the next year they started the ceremonies, the marches, to remember that day, I went proudly to them. I felt a part of it in a way that I had never felt part of something before, even our local footy team. (No wonder, kid, Jamie would've joked, given your footy skills!) And even after I heard some people saying that the landing at Anzac Cove had been a mistake, that the generals had led our boys into slaughter, even then that didn't change a thing for me. Being a hero isn't about doing great things when you're certain of winning. When the odds are good. When the stars are aligned. It's not about the glory the papers wrote about either. It's about doing the right thing by your mates. Even when death is staring you in the face. No, not even. Especially then.

That's what Snowy says. And Snowy was there.

Like Jamie. He didn't know Jamie, he was in a different battalion. But he's told me about it. Made me feel it. Understand it. See it. Feel it, in my bones. Snowy's been a soldier a long time. Comes from near Beechworth way. Ned Kelly country. (His old man knew the Kellys, in fact.) He's survived several injuries. Badly wounded at Gallipoli. Invalided to Britain. And then straight back only a few weeks later. To Belgium this time. The trenches. Got gassed there, survived that, came back for more punishment. This is the second time he's been on the Somme. All the others too, they've been in this for a good while.

Me, only two months. I couldn't join up before, though I really wanted to. Yeah, so I was too young really, only thirteen when Jamie died, but it wasn't that. I could've lied about my age. I'm big for my age, they say. Tall. Broad shoulders like me dad. Like Jamie. Can't play footy to save me life but boxing I'm pretty good at. Strong. Not scared of Jerry or anything. Wanted to fight. But I couldn't. Not with Mum the way she was.

She never got over Jamie. She had what the doctor called a breakdown. Couldn't go to work no more. Never really recovered. I had to leave school and get a job in the timber-mill, not that I minded, never much liked school. And I had to take care of her.

There was this strange thing she did, where she wanted me to read to her, from the newspapers. Though she could read perfectly well. She wanted me to read every scrap, the news, the weather report, the advertisements, every blanky thing. I didn't want to at first because the papers were of course full of news of the war and I feared it might upset her even more. But if I tried to leave that out she got angry. She would listen to the account of the battles and not say a word. Sometimes I'd make some comment on the blanky Germans or Turks or whoever and she'd nod as if she agreed but I don't think her mind was on it. I don't know where her mind was, to be honest. And when she died last year from a stroke, it was like what was started that day she got the telegram was finally ended. Like she'd been dying from that moment. Like it was almost a mercy.

I went to the recruiting office the next week. Bumped my age up two years, told 'em I was eighteen. They didn't ask too many questions. Embarked two weeks later. And so here I am now, outside VB.

'We're goin' forward.' The word's passed down the line. It's on. Jerry can't be far now, but still no artillery firing. Silently we break off into three groups, a main body heading to the town, two on the flanks to protect us and mop up Fritz outposts before they give us too much grief. I'm in the main body close to Snowy; Blue and Owl are somewhere behind us with Jimbo their other friend; and on the flanks, melting away into the darkness, Pat is with the ones who'll be making the way safe for us. Or a little safer anyway.

Closer, and we can hear fighting now as Pat's group and the others run into Fritz. We keep moving forward, bunching together because of the barbed wire fences that are everywhere, left behind by succeeding holders of the town, Fritz, the Frogs, the Poms, Fritz again, us, whoever. It's like trying to fight your way through a giant spider's web.

Suddenly, a burst of flares. Red, green, white, yellow. Someone says, and I think it's Blue, 'Hello, fireworks for Anzac Day, boys,' and that raises a laugh. But of course we know it means Fritz has heard us. Seen us. We duck down, waiting for what must come next and right on cue it does, a storm of machine-gun fire from the right of us and in front. I'm running like the others, head down, trying not to get shot or entangled in the blanky barbed wire. Behind me I hear screams, and looking back I see Blue and Owl have been hit and Jimbo's trying to help them, but I can't go back and help, now's not the time, I'm in the heart of the mob of us, Snowy at my side. And all of us with our bayonets fixed to our rifles, yelling, snarling, howling like the demons of hell or the wolves and tigers Pat spoke of earlier, we charge at the Germans.

Faintly in the distance we hear cheers from the other side of the town and know that the other Aussie brigade has heard us. Straight at the Germans we charge, and so taken aback are they by this wild onslaught that they are slow to react and when they do it's too late. I can hardly describe what happens in the next half hour or so, no quarter given on our side or theirs. Fritz fights back bravely, gunners trying to fire even when they're run through by bayonets like chickens on a spit. Sweat running down my face, I'm hardly Archie Bell from Castlemaine any more, but just part of a wild mob, parrying to left and right, trying to get in blows, to kill, to live, to win, to back up our mates.

And then I get a Jerry, straight through the heart, a lucky blow, despite my wild thrust, and I see his eyes stare at me bewildered as he falls. His eyes are blue, the exact shade of Jamie's, and though this is not the first time I have killed a man in battle it is the first time at such close quarters, and for a heartbeat I feel that knowledge rise in my gorge like sick.

But there's no time to think. Our rush has been so fast that we are too far in VB too soon and have to pull back a little. But the Germans in the town have seen what's happened, and from then on they start surrendering. Dozens of them, soon hundreds, so many prisoners that it becomes an embarrassment. They've got to be parked somewhere out of harm's way – the order's been given now we must take as many prisoners as we can – till the die-hard resisters and the snipers who've holed up behind rubble and in ruined buildings can be dealt with.

That's what Snowy's sent to do, pick off snipers – he's a blanky good shot – but yours truly is put on guard duty, the last thing I want to do. I try to argue with the officer but he's in no mood to listen, and so I have to march off with three of our blokes and this column of dejected, ashen-faced Jerries to wait in a safe spot in the fields till the all-clear is given.

I'm simmering with annoyance at the thought I have to play nanny to this bunch while my mates are still out there fighting. That blanky officer knows I'm younger than the others. Less experienced. In his mind that qualifies me for the soft jobs.

'Cos the Jerry prisoners are not going to be a problem any time soon. They look exhausted. Broken down. Some of them are wounded but only slightly – the really injured ones have been stretchered off, like our wounded. Their uniforms are dirty, stained, their eyes are empty. Crack Bavarian and

Prussian troops were supposed to be stationed here, we were told. Well, these fellas don't look like crack anything, except cracked in spirit. They've given up. They don't look at me but stare at the ground.

Time passes. Dawn breaks, the sun rises, the day advances. Dimly in the town behind us we can hear the occasional crack of a rifle or a burst of machine-gun fire but it's getting fewer. More prisoners join our lot. They all sit there, staring at the ground.

I wonder what they're thinking. Your average Jerry is a fanatic, I've read. Thinks his race are supermen. Some supermen, this lot! My mind skitters around. If the Jerries hadn't started the war then I wouldn't be here. Owl and Blue'd be safe with their families. Snowy would've taken up that job as a horse trainer, become a big shot. Jamie wouldn't be dead. Mum would still be alive. I'd have a home. A family. I'd have trained to be a real proper boxer in Melbourne, I'd had offers. I might have a girl too. A pretty thing with long curls like my favourite film star, Lilian Gish. We would go around town with her on my arm and go to restaurants and the picture theatre and on Melbourne Cup Day we'd go to the races with Mum and Jamie down from the country, and we'd pick the winner. Which would be the horse Snowy had trained. We'd win big, there'd be champagne and cake and everything would be...

What the blanky blanky are you doing? hisses a voice in my ear. It's Stevie, the one in charge of guard duty. Keep yer eyes open, mate.

Eh? What's he talking about? I've not been asleep. I glare at him but he doesn't care. Get up, have a walk around, he orders, as though he's an officer or somethin'. Which he isn't, just some cocky farmer from way out in the Mallee.

I shrug to show how much I give about his orders, but I get up anyway because it doesn't look good in front of the prisoners to be arguing. I walk up and down and as I do I happen to see one of the prisoners staring at me. He's small and dark and though he has a little moustache it's clear he's pretty young. I give him a glare to let him know I'm watching him and he better not be up to any tricks, but he gives me this little gesture which looks like he's waving me over. You have to be joking. If I'm not taking orders from some Mallee cocky, I'm sure not taking any from a blanky Fritz.

I see his mouth form a word. Please. Not *bitte*, which I know is German for please, but the good old English please. The magic word, Mum always said.

What's the magic word, boys? she'd say to Jamie and me.

Yeah, what, I say.

Please, he says, will you come here?

I look at Stevie. He shrugs. Go ahead.

I go over to the bloke. What'd you want? I say roughly.

He reaches inside his uniform pocket and pulls out a crumpled letter. He looks at me, tries a little smile. For my girl, yes? You post this for me.

I'm not your blanky postman, I tell him harshly and he smiles again, Please, just a small thing. I look at him, at the hopeful smile, the outstretched hand with the letter, and something snaps in me. I leap at him, knocking the letter flying, grabbing him by the throat. Then I'm pulled off him and Stevie's bellowing, Cripes, you mad beggar, what are you doin'? And he's shoving me away, to sprawl in the grass.

I thought he was going to go for me, I manage to lie, but Stevie shakes his head. You're touched, mate, he says, now pull yerself together or yer'll end up in the clink. Prisoners is prisoners, see, you don't hurt them, not unless you want our blokes to be hurt too.

I know that. I know all that. Shame is washing over me in cold crinkles of skin. Jeez, I'm not that sort. Not the kind that would go for an unarmed bloke. I want to explain. But I can't. The words

247

won't come. I can't say how looking at that letter of his, and the smile, it felt like he was mocking me. Like underneath he was laughing at me, at us all. Owl and Blue are dead and Jamie and Mum and countless many more and for an instant, to me, that bloke he looked like the one who done them all in. I know that's mad. I know it is, but I hated him more in that moment than I hated the one I'd killed back there, the one with the blue eyes like Jamie's. I wanted him to pay. I wanted someone to pay. Some bastard Jerry would-be superman. But now I look at the bloke and all I see is a frightened kid trying to look like a man, and I feel sick to my stomach.

You goin' to behave now, cobber, asks Stevie, not unkindly, and I nod. Get away over the other side, then, he says, and I nod again. I'm about to go when I hesitate. Part of me wants to go to the prisoner and say – what? An apology? That would stick in my craw. No. I can't say anything. There is nothing to say. I'm turning away when I hear this whisper from him, hoarse, because of his throat which must be sore. He's got the letter back in his hand, all dusty from the ground. Please, he says, very quietly.

I stare at him. He looks back. I can't say what it is he has in his eyes. I can't read people that well. But our eyes meet, just for that instant. Without a word, I nod, take that letter, and walk away, to the other side of the group of prisoners. There is such an ache in my chest. A feeling that grips me tight, like the killing fury, like the pain of memory. Cripes, it's too big for me. The pity of it all.

THE DAY THE WAR ENDED
Leslie Wilson

Author's note:

My English grandfather was too old to fight in World War One, but my German grandfather was a teenage soldier from 1916 to 1918 and my grandmother was a teenager during the war, like Gabi in my story. My grandmother's brother Leo had his head shot off at Verdun, like the Leo of the story. I wanted to describe how that horror would affect a young girl, and show how the post-war democracy was tainted in the minds of many Germans by the humiliation of the surrender.

Prenzlauer Berg District, Berlin
Friday 8th November 1918

After school we queue for food.[1] Once upon a time, before the war, the kids used to come home and do their homework in the afternoons, and play. Now the most important thing is queueing, because everyone has to eat and there isn't much to go round – except turnips. I get onto the end of the queue for bread; Mother's in the milk queue, round the corner. Old Rosi, our maid, is trying to get fats. It's raw cold and drizzling with rain.

'Hello, Gabi!'

It's Lukas Hoffmann. He smiles at me, and I feel warm all of a sudden. I only hope he thinks it's the cold that has made my cheeks go pink.

His mother's not in any queue. He lives in the poor houses at the back court, behind ours, and Frau Hoffmann works all night making munitions, so she's asleep now. She'll wake up and get the family dinner before she leaves for the factory tonight. The working-class women round here are mainly at the munitions factories.

---

1 German schools used to all start at eight and finish at one pm, Monday to Saturday.

Lukas is fourteen, just like me, and he's clever; clever enough to get a scholarship to the grammar school. We all used to play together when we were small, because Mother isn't a snob.

'Do you think we'll get any bread?' he asks.

I say: 'While there's life, there's hope,' and he laughs.

'A bit of bread makes the turnip soup go down better,' he says.

He's thinner than he should be – I reckon his family have half as many turnips in their watery soup as we do. But I've started to notice how nice-looking he is, and what a lovely smile he's got. I'm glad he laughed at my joke.

And then suddenly a man comes past the queue, swinging himself on his crutches, shouting: 'The Emperor's abdicated!'

There's a silence, then everyone is talking.

Lukas says: 'If he's gone – then there'll be peace, won't there? And your brother will come home. Only—'

Only my other brother won't come home and Lukas's brother has lost an arm, and nothing can change those things.

I remember when it all started, four years ago. Leo, all excited, saying: 'We're mobilising. Goodbye, school, I'm off to the Champs Elysées!'

Mother's face went white, but Leo picked me up and swung me round. I was excited too. I shrieked happily.

'We're going to Paris, to Paris, to Paris!' Leo called out. And then he looked at our dead father's photograph and said: 'I'll make you proud of me.'

Paul was really fed up. 'Why aren't I old enough?' he complained. 'It'll all be over before I'm seventeen.'

Leo and Erich, Lukas's brother, went off to the war together in the autumn. Erich was another scholarship boy, and Leo's best friend.

We were all there, pinning flowers to our brave soldiers' uniforms. We'd bought red roses for Leo. Lukas and his mother gave Erich geraniums from their window box. Herr Hoffmann was dead like my father; killed in an accident at the brewery where he worked.

There was a band playing, and the boys' faces were bright – noble, I thought.

Only Paul was sulking because he couldn't go yet.

'It's a shame,' Leo said to him. 'You'd fight well, I know.'

Paul almost cheered up.

'Only,' Leo said, 'it is all going to be over by Christmas. We're going to steamroller the French.

But you can probably do things to help the war effort at home.'

Paul didn't look very pleased with Leo's kindness.

'The war might make us better,' Mother said when we got home. 'All those men willing to sacrifice their lives – and we wives and mothers, we have to be willing to sacrifice them, only I've always taken such care of Leo—'

Her face went all crumpled and she ran off to cry. But I wouldn't cry. Leo would get to Paris and it'd all be over by Christmas.

Ha, ha.

They needed teachers at the primary school because the men who were old enough to fight had joined up. Mother had been a teacher before she got married, so she went to work there. We were all working like mad on the Home Front. Paul and I took most of our kitchen pots and pans to be made into guns, and I learned to knit for Leo – things to keep him warm in winter: a balaclava, gloves, socks and a scarf.

Leo was killed in 1916, at Verdun. Killed instantly, they said. And I'd loved him so much, he was so sweet and kind and made a special pet of me.

Mother went on teaching. She said it helped her,

having a job to do. But sometimes she'd go into Leo's room and sit on the bed and I heard her sobbing. Then I'd go in there too and put my arms round her, and cry with her, and she said I was a comfort.

'And we have to be brave,' she'd say, 'because he was willing to make that sacrifice. Only, maybe – it's harder for us who are left behind. No! I shouldn't talk like that.'

She smiled rather desperately, all over her wet face, and I made myself smile back.

Now Leo's photograph stood next to Father's on the mantelpiece, and we took turns to find flowers to put in the vase in front of them both. But Father died when I was too young to remember him. It was Leo I missed, so very dreadfully.

And then Paul told lies to the recruiting board, and they let him join up. He was only sixteen, a year underage.

We got a letter from him this morning, but a letter doesn't mean he's alive. The last letter from Leo came the day he was killed, and we were happy, because we thought he was all right. It was two days before we got the official letter, telling us he was dead. Mother keeps it behind his photograph. We've read it to ragged shreds.

* * *

Lukas's brother appears, holding a milk can in the hand he has left. He's got a grey scarf round his neck to keep him warm. His mother knitted it for him when he was still at the front. Erich is back at school now, studying for his Abitur.[2] Only it's tough for him, because he's had to learn to write left-handed.

'Have you heard the news?' he says to us. 'The people have got rid of the Emperor. Now we can end the war.'

I can't imagine it. 'No Emperor,' I say. 'He's always been – so important. We called him the All-Highest, didn't we? And we sang that song, "Hail to you, in your victory wreath".'

Erich shakes his head at me. 'There's no victory wreath for him now.'

Old Dr Mansfeld, the retired lawyer, is standing just ahead of us in the queue. He turns on Erich, shaking his silver-topped cane. 'Are you glad, young man? Dishonour, that's what it means. The Bavarians turning against their King, workers' councils' – he says that as if the words tasted disgusting – 'taking over our cities. Mob rule, I call it. And those sailors in Kiel, refusing to go out and engage the British – it's appalling. We should fight to the death.'

---

2 Like the French Baccalauréat.

Erich turns on him. 'It's easy for old men to talk – you weren't out there in the mud. Honour? There wasn't even decency. Rats, filth, stinking corpses—'

'You know I gave my son,' the old man says harshly, like a crow. 'My only son.'

Erich shakes his empty jacket-sleeve at the old man.

'This is what I gave – no, what was stolen from me. My arm, my right arm. And I lost my best friend.' Erich glances at me.

I remember his happy, lit-up face when he went away with Leo, to fight. I remember the red roses on Leo's chest – like blood, I think suddenly.

I start to chew my thumbnail. Mother would tell me off, but I can't help it.

'If we surrender,' I say, and stop. It's hard to put it into words. 'Leo sacrificed his life for our cause – and that'd be wasted, if we give up—'

'Yes,' says Mansfeld to Erich. 'Listen to this girl!'

Erich bites his lip. Then he says: 'And your other brother? Paul? Would you be happy to sacrifice him?' His voice is bitterly sarcastic.

'I wasn't happy about Leo!' Now I'm crying. It's not just about Leo, I've suddenly realised.

Leo was the big brother I adored, almost like a father, I think. But Paul and I – we used to raid the larder for raisins when Rosi was out. He used to annoy me – like when he said noodles were worms, and we fought, but he never really hurt me. And we used to scream with laughter at silly things – I've never had quite as much fun laughing with anyone else.

If Paul was killed, I'd lose part of myself.

'Leave her alone,' Lukas says to his brother.

'It's not true,' Mother says miserably, when we all get home. 'They want the Emperor to abdicate, but he won't. So Paul has to keep on fighting.'

I'm so worried and upset and muddled I can't hug her, to comfort her. I feel dreadful, but I run away to my room and shut myself in there.

I think about Leo's death. I always imagine him running towards the enemy with that noble look on his face, and suddenly he falls, but his face is still alight, happy. He was a hero.

But maybe one hero is enough in a family? And it's two years since anyone seriously talked about winning the war.

Saturday 9th November

It's foggy as well as cold now; we shiver at our desks because there's no heating nowadays. At the end of school our teachers tell us there are massive demonstrations going on, and we have to go straight home (like good girls) and stay in so as not to worry our mothers.

But if I want to get the tram home, I'd have to cross Rosenthal Street, and one of the demonstrations is going along there. I can't do anything but stand waiting for it to go past, which could take hours. The fog clings to my coat and damps my scarf; that's uncomfortable, but I'd be colder if I took the scarf off.

It's mainly men marching up out of the fog; some of them are still in uniform – soldiers, sailors. Some of them have guns. Some of them are older men, workers, and there are women too. Red flags waving, for revolution. They're singing. Not the songs about winning the war, still less 'Hail to you, in your victory wreath', but a song I've never heard before.

I catch bits of the words – about wage-slaves being drained of blood by rich people who don't care about them; about the people breaking their chains.

Someone nudges me. I look round, and it's Lukas, with his school bag on his back.

'I'm going with them!' he yells in my ear.

He must agree with the marchers – well, why wouldn't he? Frau Hoffmann works really hard, but even before the war she could never make ends meet properly. And the skinny clever Hoffmann boys were graciously picked out to get an education, but they have to coach stupid rich kids when they should be doing their own work. Just to get a few more turnips in the soup.

And partly because of the way I like him nowadays, partly just because I'm sick of standing still and I do want to see what happens, I go along too.

So now I'm marching in a demonstration. And now the song is about soldiers chucking their guns down because they don't want to kill the working people on the other side.

That sounds good, because of Paul. Only – French working men came into Germany with Napoleon and looted and murdered. Leo told me the French have been invading German lands for centuries – till we united and got strong enough to beat them. And what will happen if we surrender now?

I'm marching in a demonstration, and I don't know if I agree with it. Just to see what happens, and because of a boy I like. This is crazy. I ought to go home. But my feet keep walking forward. I hear Lukas beside me, singing the chorus with the rest:

THE DAY THE WAR ENDED

'So comrades, come rally
    And the last fight let us face
    The Internationale unites the human race!'

Nobody notices that I'm not singing.

The word's going round again: 'The Emperor has abdicated! Pass it on!'

Lukas says: 'That's what we heard yesterday, and—'

No, this time it's true!' says a man in a shabby waistcoat, and he takes his bowler hat off and waves it in the air.

Now everyone's cheering, and shouting: 'To the Parliament building!'

'Not that it's ever been a real Parliament,' Lukas says, or rather yells to be heard. 'Not with the Emperor and his Chancellor calling all the shots. Only that's over now. Finished. Can you believe it? Now the people will have a real voice.'

We're in the big space in front of the Tiergarten Park, between the Royal Palace and the German Parliament building. The fog is lifting and I see thousands of people around me, men and women and kids like us. I'm squeezed up close to Lukas – which is lovely, but a bit distracting.

Now there's a group of men coming out onto the

balcony. The people in the huge crowd are cheering again and waving hats.

'Scheidemann,' they shout. 'Scheidemann!'

He's one of the Social Democrats, the new government.

Scheidemann talks about the war, about the cruel sacrifices people have made. He says it's over.

I can't believe it. Have the guns stopped? Is Paul safe? Is he still alive? Oh, he must be.

I hear Scheidemann talking about the royalists who've stamped on democracy for years and years, saying: 'These enemies of the people have been dealt with now, I hope for ever. The Emperor has abdicated.' But that doesn't matter as much to me as Paul does.

Scheidemann has to stop talking, because of the roar that goes up when he says the Emperor has really abdicated. Hats in the air again, people hugging each other, people crying. I'm crying. And Lukas puts his arm round me and squeezes me tight – and then he kisses my cheek.

Now I'm so happy! Lukas has kissed me – though maybe it's only because he's excited – but I don't think so, somehow. And suddenly I'm sure Paul's alive, and safe.

Scheidemann talks about challenges ahead, but he tells us it is all for the people's good. 'The old, crumbling monarchy has collapsed,' he calls out. 'Long live the new! Long live the German republic!

Lukas turns to me, and the next moment we're kissing properly. It's wonderful, his lips on mine – and I can't look at him, but when the kiss is over he takes my hand and holds it tight, and I can't say how lovely that feels.

I see the soldiers in the crowd, pulling the cockades off their caps and laughing, and that's when I think of Leo again. He was laughing when he went away to war, laughing at the idea of facing death. Herr Scheidemann talked about cruel sacrifices, and losing Leo felt cruel, I know, but it was a willing, joyful sacrifice that my hero brother made – and Paul was so keen to play his part, he joined up a year early. If peace means my brothers are defeated—

Suddenly I'm not happy at all.

'I'd better go home,' I say, 'or I'll be in trouble.'

Of course, Mother asks me where I've been – and I feel as if I had marks from Lukas's kisses printed on my cheek and my lips, and she'll see them – and she thinks I'm far too young for stuff with boys. I don't want her forbidding me to see Lukas.

I tell her I met him and we got swept up in the demonstration – there's no point in telling complicated lies. And I tell her how I heard

Scheidemann announce the Republic.

She only says: 'It's all very well for politicians to say the war is over. They haven't signed an armistice yet.'

'You mean, they have to go on fighting?'

She nods unhappily. 'Right till the last minute.'

Later, we hear a faint rattle of gunfire coming from the town centre. Why's there fighting here?

The sound gets into my dreams, and I think I'm in a trench beside Paul in France. Then he gets up and starts collecting his kit. 'You stay here. I've got to go and fight. Right till the last minute.' I want to come too, but he won't let me. 'This is boys' stuff,' he says, just as he used to when I wanted to play with his toy soldiers.

I wake up; they're still firing. I go to the window and stare out, but all I can see is the fuzz of fog. The window feels very cold when I touch it.

I can hardly believe Lukas kissed me yesterday. Maybe that was a dream too. Everything seems strange, frightening, uncertain.

Sunday 10th November

You can still hear gunfire, all the time, and it's still foggy. Frau Dresner from downstairs comes to see Mother, and she says it's the royalists who want to sabotage the Revolution. Herr Dresner knows; he's a journalist.

'But an editor, thank goodness,' she says. 'He doesn't have to go out and report on the fighting.'

Mother goes into the kitchen to get imitation coffee for Frau Dresner. Rosi makes it out of toasted bread-ends.

I say: 'Can I go out?' I want to be sure what happened yesterday wasn't a dream.

'Where?' Mother asks sharply. 'I don't want you going down into the city.'

I shake my head. 'Lukas was going to explain some maths to me.'

'Don't go onto the street!' Mother says. 'And make sure you wrap up warmly!'

As if I was a little kid! But as I go out, I hear Frau Dresner say: 'They grow up fast, nowadays.'

She's noticed. She sounds amused, friendly, but I wish she hadn't said anything. I hang around by the door, listening for what Mother will say.

She answers very quietly, but I hear her. 'No, she's young for her age. They're just like brother and sister, and she misses Paul so much—'

I slip away. It's good if she thinks I'm so young for my age – but annoying too.

Lukas isn't in the courtyard. I walk through at the back, towards the rear court, where he lives in a poor people's flats area. I'm thinking again that maybe kissing Lukas was a dream. Probably he's gone off with some other boys – or maybe even another girl.

'Gabi!'

He's there, and his smile tells me it's OK. We walk around the courtyard for half an hour and talk, but we can't hold hands or kiss because of all the people watching.

'Is the war ever going to end?' I ask him.

'I don't know.'

I don't know why I expected him to know.

You can still hear them shooting, down in the city centre.

Monday 11th November

My school, and Lukas's, are closed because of the unrest. They don't want the boys and girls getting shot – or joining in the fighting. Mother's primary school is open, though, because it's just nearby and nobody's fighting up here. It's still foggy.

So Lukas and I have to queue in the morning, along with other grammar school kids and the usual ladies and maidservants and old men. The munitions factories are still working, though everyone says we must get news of the ceasefire today.

I so wish I knew about Paul! It's so awful not knowing. Like torture.

Lukas understands that, but I can't let him hold my hand, because of all the neighbours who might tell Mother.

And then Dr Mansfeld appears and he's crying. He's walking down the street, with the tears pouring down his old cheeks and catching in his moustache and beard.

'I said so,' he calls out to everyone. 'I knew it would mean shame and dishonour for us. These Socialists—'

As he reads the headlines aloud, the queue dissolves; it's just a crowd, standing round Mansfeld, listening – and soon he's not the only one crying. It's awful.

'We must give up five thousand cannons, thirty-thousand machine guns, three thousand trench mortars, two thousand planes.' Mansfeld's voice shakes. 'We must give up the left bank of the Rhine, and the cities of Mainz, Coblenz, Cologne, and all the way down the right bank there must be a neutral zone. We must leave the factories and railways intact on the left bank – for the French to plunder. We must give them five thousand locomotives, a hundred and fifty thousand railway coaches, and ten thousand trucks. We must have enemy troops occupying the whole of our country. We must send back their prisoners of war, but they won't promise to return ours. We must give up our battleships, and the rest of the fleet must be disarmed and controlled by the enemy—'

We'll be trampled on, humiliated.

'We'll be defenceless,' someone calls out.

'Yes,' says Mansfeld furiously. 'Stripped of our honour and our army. And what will happen to our economy without the factories around the Rhine? We have been betrayed. Betrayed, remember that!'

He stands there, cursing the Socialists, and Erich appears, just like on Friday, and he's carrying a paper too. Erich starts shouting back at Mansfeld, saying it was the Emperor's fault, he'd wanted the war in the first place.

'This whole country has been run by the military,' he says, 'for the military. If we'd held back in 1914, if we'd let the Austrians get on with it—'

'They were our allies,' someone yells. 'And you were glad enough to go.'

'I learned my mistake.'

But I'm thinking of Leo. My lovely big brother, who gave up his life so that this shouldn't happen. And Paul, risking his life. It does feel as if they've been betrayed.

But the queue forms up again, because everyone needs milk. People are still crying and arguing and yelling at each other, though. Erich and Mansfeld have both disappeared. I don't know where they went.

Lukas and I walk through the fog to the bread queue; we get bread, but when we go to the shop for fats, they're finished. The fog is suddenly much thicker, and we walk into it, because then nobody can see if we hold hands. We don't talk, and we don't kiss either. I don't feel like kissing. I feel numb, and I think he does too. Only once, I say:

'Scheidemann must have known this when he talked about challenges. Couldn't they get a better settlement?'

'Only by fighting on,' Lukas says grimly.

Then Johann Schmidt comes towards us out of the fog. A small, intense boy with wire glasses on his face, who's in Lukas's class. We let go of each other quickly, but I don't think he cares.

'Have you heard?' he asks. 'The armistice conditions?'

We nod.

'There'll have to be another war,' Johann says. 'Then we can thrash them.' He walks off, as if he doesn't want an answer.

I hear a clock strike. The armistice is due to be signed at eleven. I listen, counting the strokes.

'That's it,' Lukas says, when the bell stops. 'The war is over.'

I feel that torturing hope and fear again.

'Paul!' I say. 'Lukas, I have to go home.'

'If you want to.' He sounds disappointed.

'I know it's stupid – but I want to see if there's a letter saying Paul is – you know. If there isn't, maybe—'

'Yes,' he says at once. 'Let's go.'

He comes with me to the letter boxes in the hallway. The post has come, but nothing from the army – and I don't feel as safe as I hoped. The letter might get here tomorrow, or the next day. If the victors let the post go through. They might enjoy leaving German families in torment.

I turn away from the letter box. Erich is coming again.

'Are you all right?' he asks me.

'She's worried about Paul,' Lukas says.

Erich says, 'I hope he's survived.' He looks edgy, tired. He has a lot of pain from his missing arm, Lukas told me, and he gets stressed. I wonder how many other arguments he's had this morning.

Shakily, I say, 'Having one brother die a hero's death is enough for me.'

'A hero's death!' Erich's face changes, he looks

half crazy. 'Listen, Gabi. I was there. I saw your brother die.'

I'm suddenly dreadfully scared of him. I want to shut him up. 'He was killed instantly. They told us. He didn't suffer,' I say.

'Killed instantly, yes. The shell that took my arm, it shot his head off.'

I feel sick. I'm going to be sick.

Lukas puts his arm round me and shouts at his brother. 'If you could hold your tongue about that for three years, why not hold it for ever?'

Erich doesn't seem to hear. 'I dream about it, night after night. Sometimes I see it in the daytime too. Leo's head exploded. Some of it splashed me—'

I mustn't throw up, not with food so scarce. I hate being sick anyway, it's horrible.

As horrible as Leo's death, that I've been fooling myself about. There was no noble expression on his face because he didn't have a face left.

Now I'm standing right in front of Erich. 'You should have told us!' I say. 'You should have told us long ago.' I turn away, but I take Lukas's hand and squeeze it, so he knows I'm not angry with him. I go upstairs.

I'm in Leo's room. There are his school books, his civilian clothes hanging in the wardrobe, waiting for

Paul when – or if – he comes back. I go on into Paul's room and look at his books and clothes, and the toy soldiers he never let me play with. They're wood, not lead, so they didn't go to be melted down. Father carved them years ago, when Leo was small.

'Paul! I whisper. 'Are you alive?'

I listen hard, desperate to hear his voice come across the hundreds of kilometres, but I don't. I've never felt so alone in my whole life. And I think of old Mansfeld crying.

Then I think how for more than four years the whole world, almost, has been pouring all its energy and work and everything it has into killing. About the millions of young men and boys, all of them terribly important to someone, who are gone for ever. They should have been alive, I think. They should have been alive.

I remember Johann Schmidt saying: 'There'll have to be another war.' I imagine him marching to war, and Lukas having to go. And then it happens. I can smell the front: the sharp whiff of explosive that catches at the top of my nose, and the awful smell of dead bodies. And I can feel Paul, as if he was standing beside me. He's desperately tired.

'Gabi,' his voice comes. He's almost bewildered. 'The guns have stopped and I'm alive. I can't believe it, but it's all over.' And then, fiercely: 'Gabi, I don't want to see the toy soldiers when I come home. Get rid of them.'

'Yes.' I know he can hear me. 'Paul, I love you. I can't wait to see you again.'

'I can't wait to see all of you too.'

Then he's gone, and all I can smell is the room. But I know it's been real. And I can still feel Paul's weariness. He must be sick in his soul, because of all the things he's been through at the front.

But now he's coming home, and when it's a nice day we'll go to the lake at Müggelsee and walk along the sandy beach where we used to play when we were kids. I'll do silly things and make him laugh. I'll help him learn to be happy again.

But he mustn't see those toy soldiers.

I pick them up in handfuls, gather my skirt up and dump them there; I run to the kitchen.

Rosi's there, peeling turnips.

'Gabi!' she says. 'What have you got in your skirt?'

I open the stove door. 'We need fuel, don't we? To cook the soup?'

'Gabi, those are Paul's soldiers!'

'He doesn't want them. I know.'

She gives me an odd, scared look. 'He's alive,' I say quickly. 'He – he just spoke to me and told me so.'

She believes in that kind of thing – but I know she's afraid to believe that I'm right.

I'm certain, though. She'll see, when he comes home.

I toss them in and see the flames take them. Mother said I was young for my age, but now I feel a hundred years old.

I say: 'It's time to stop playing with soldiers.'

THE UNKNOWN SOLDIER
Paul Dowswell

Author's note:

*I have always been haunted by the First World War.
My story here was inspired by recent reading about soldiers
who had survived the war but had been left with deep
psychological damage.*

The Maudsley Military Hospital, London
10th November 1920, 10pm

John sometimes wondered what his real name was. As he lay there in the ward after lights out, trying not to fall asleep, he could recall with crystal clarity conversations that had happened over the past year. But before that, before he'd gone to the nerve hospital, there was a great black hole. He could remember odd snatches of his previous life, usually in dreams, but he didn't want to think about what had happened to him before he came to the Maudsley. It was all too disturbing...

One conversation he remembered was making him particularly indignant that evening. Two doctors had had a discussion right in front of him, about what they would call him. It had happened just a few days after he'd arrived.

They had started off using words he didn't understand, like 'dissociative generalised amnesia', and 'psychogenic'. He'd become familiar with those words now, having heard them many times, but he still didn't know what they meant. Then there was another word they used which he did understand – *malingering* – which made him squirm.

They had begun to talk about what they ought to

call him. One of them suggested 'William', having recently read in the *Times* that it was the most common name for men of the patient's age, which they had estimated at no more than eighteen. 'At least we've got a good chance of getting it right,' he joked.

But the other doctor didn't like that. 'My father's called William,' he said stuffily. 'I wouldn't want to give that name to this unhappy specimen.'

John could feel his anger rising but he thought it best to say nothing. If these men thought he really was a malingerer they might have him shot. That's what had happened to some of the men, before all this…when was it…he shuddered and tried to blank it out.

'Then we shall call him John,' said the first doctor. He looked over his spectacles and spoke to his patient for the first time: 'Is that all right, old chap? Will John do for you?'

'I suppose so, sir,' he had said, trying to hide his hostility.

He'd got used to it now. John was a solid, decent name. It would do fine. John was one of the apostles and one of the gospels. He was also one of the Kings of England, even if he was a bad 'un, so he dimly remembered from school. He must have gone to school if he was remembering things like that. But when he tried to picture where, and who with, his heart started to thump, and his ears started to whistle and there was all this static running around his head – the sort of hiss you sometimes heard on the telephone, only much louder.

John could stay awake no longer. As he watched the shadows drift across the length of the ward, his exhausted eyes lost focus and he was falling, falling down a black hole.

Sitting at the end of the ward, on a desk with a small reading lamp, Annie Scott looked up from her book and muttered a choice swear word under her breath. She had never heard words like that, let alone used them, before she started working with soldiers. She knew at once who was making a disturbance. It was John. 'The Great Mystery', they called him.

She'd read his doctors' notes when no one else was around and they'd thought at first he was 'swinging the lead', another term she had recently learned. But over the last few months they'd all become convinced he really didn't have the first idea who he actually was. Just recently the doctors had been making ominous suggestions in their notes about sending him to a long-term asylum, as there was nothing more they could do for him at the Maudsley. Annie had worked in places like that when she was doing her training, and she shuddered at the thought. John was not one of those hopeless cases who perpetually rocked to and fro in their bed, or stared at a fixed spot in ominous silence, or raged and wailed against the world as they tore at their clothes or hair. He wouldn't ever get better in a place like that.

Annie had suggested they send a letter about him to the newspapers, along with a photograph. Maybe his mum would recognise him. But no one was interested. There were thousands of sob stories after the war. Poor John was just another one.

Now here he was again, crying and shouting in that funny Northern accent, disturbing the other patients on the ward. He was having one of those peculiar one-way conversations. 'Harry, you've got to stick with me. Stay as close as you can.' 'Get down, Harry, can't you hear me?' 'Harry, crawl along the ditch!' It was like listening to someone on the phone. Only John was calling out to the other side rather than someone on the end of the line.

She hurried to his bed. 'Come on, John, you're waking them all up,' she whispered. 'Calm yourself, Sonny Jim.' She held his hand and stayed with him until he settled down. They used to ask him what he was dreaming about when he'd first arrived. Some of the dreams he remembered, and they were there in his notes. He'd told the doctors about one where he was trapped in a shell crater with a ticking shell about to go off, and every time he tried to get out machine-gun bullets peppered the ground around him. There was another one too, where he was in a dark place, a cave maybe, standing in front of a wooden ladder and waiting for a whistle to blow. When it did, he knew he had to climb that ladder and he knew that something terrifying was waiting for him at the top.

It was the dreams about Harry that really puzzled the doctors. You always knew when he had them because he'd call out that name. When they asked him about them, after he'd woken up, he didn't remember a thing. Annie had a nagging suspicion it was better that way. Maybe whatever was haunting the poor lad was best kept in the dark.

She had to admit she'd taken quite a shine to him. He was a handsome boy, despite the crease in the forehead where it looked like he'd caught a bit of shrapnel. They thought maybe that's what had caused the amnesia – that inability to remember who he was – but the x-rays had shown there were no splinters to remove.

It was funny, she thought; when he was awake, when he wasn't having those dreams, he was lovely – usually cheerful, ever helpful. The way he spoke reminded her of her friend Lizzie Kirke. She was from Preston – somewhere up in Lancashire. They had done their nursing training together in London. She'd gone back up there but they still wrote to each other. She worked in a retreat for soldiers like John. Maybe one day she'd go and visit.

This John liked to read too – anything from before the war. But anything about the war, that was out of the question. She'd seen it happen. The shaking, the sweating. He changed colour before your eyes – a ghastly pallor. It said in his notes that they'd found him wandering on the outskirts of a village behind the lines, a week or two before the end of the war. Ragged uniform hanging off him, no identity papers or tags. He was lucky not to be shot for desertion. But whoever made these decisions had decided he really didn't have a clue who he was. And after a few months he was transferred to the Maudsley. That's where most of the shell-shock men were sent.

He'd recently been reading Robert Louis Stevenson. She had promised to take him down to the library the following afternoon and see if they could find another one, or a Trollope or Jules Verne. Something gentle, with nothing too unpleasant. Or maybe some poems. She thought he'd like a bit of poetry.

* * *

John tried to get back to sleep, but after an hour he gave up. He was glad the nice nurse had woken him. That other one that sometimes did the night shift, Nurse Stamp, she would scold him when she had to wake him up. Tell him that was not how a man behaved. This one, Nurse Scott, she would stroke his hand and whisper. Coax him out of his nightmare.

He got up and went to the day room to make himself a cup of tea. The last embers of the fire still glowed in the hearth, so he guessed it must be the middle of the night. Nurse Stamp wouldn't let him go there until after breakfast. She said it was against regulations. But Nurse Scott, she turned a blind eye. There'd be no one important around until seven o'clock, she said, so she didn't mind as long as he was back in his bed by then. Sometimes she even came in to keep him company for a while. He knew her first name; Annie, it was. He liked that name.

She came in a few minutes later. 'Just time for a quick cup of tea,' she whispered, as she picked up a newspaper. 'Don't tell anyone, will you, John? I should be there in the ward all night, but everything's quiet and I can hear if there's any trouble if I keep the door open. And I'm really struggling to keep awake.' She opened the paper. 'Look at this,' she said. 'The paper's full of the Unknown Soldier.

They've chosen someone at random from all those poor souls they buried out in France in the mass graves, not knowing who they were. It's all here, do you want to read about it?'

She knew he didn't like to see anything about the war, but she kept thinking about what the doctors were threatening to do. They said he needed to confront what was frightening him so much, and every so often she thought she ought to try.

John shook his head. He was starting to feel really uneasy. But she carried on talking. He wanted to tell her to stop, but he didn't like to offend her. And he had to admit, he was actually curious about this.

'They've put him in an ancient oak coffin and taken him from Boulogne to Dover,' she said, 'and he's come up to London on a train decked out with purple cloth and chrysanthemums. He's being buried this morning at Westminster Abbey. He'll be there among the Kings and Queens and the war heroes and the poets.'

John didn't say anything, and she stopped talking after that. Maybe she could see how uncomfortable she was making him. But he had to admit, it was a good idea. Making that soldier stand for the thousands of poor sods who were buried in unmarked graves because nobody knew who they were.

Annie went back to the ward after that, and soon

after his eyes started to droop. He crept back to bed and remembered she'd promised to take him to the local library the following afternoon. She was coming in especially early, before her night shift. He thought that was really grand of her.

The Strand, London
11th November 1920, 10.30am
Standing on the grand avenue of the Mall, Tom and Edie Spencer craned their necks over the hushed crowd to see the coffin go by. They were three rows from the front, with maybe six or seven rows behind them. Edie was glad they had got there early. They had taken the train down from Preston the previous night and stayed with friends in Finsbury Park. There must be hundreds of thousands of people out on the route now. Most were wearing black armbands.

Placed on a gun carriage pulled by six black horses, and shrouded with a muddy Union Jack, the coffin of the Unknown Warrior had his ragged uniform webbing and his dented Brodie helmet placed on top. Seeing these personal items brought a raw intimacy to the dead soldier, and Edie reached for her husband's hand.

It was a beautiful, gentle autumn day but the air was dense like a thunderstorm, thick with grief.

There were a few sobs as the carriage passed, but most of the crowd stayed silent, save for the rustling of clothing as hats were taken from heads.

Edie whispered to Tom that she felt Albert was very near, and like every other parent in the crowd she told herself that perhaps it was her boy in that coffin.

The Maudsley Hospital
11th November 1920, 3.30pm
It was a short walk from the hospital to the library, but on the way they came across a noisy protest by unemployed soldiers and sailors. They were carrying placards demanding jobs, and what was really odd was that they were all clad in skirts, dresses and big hats to demonstrate their feelings: they were being treated worse than women, they said. John was glad they weren't wearing uniforms. He always felt anxious when he saw a soldier in uniform.

Whenever he went outside the hospital he always felt self-conscious about his scar and the way it distorted his face. He thought everyone would stare at him. But at least his wound wasn't as bad as some of the men he saw out in the street. Some of them wore flesh-painted tin plates on their faces to cover the disfiguring holes and damaged tissue of their injuries.

Annie took him into the library, suggested he have a look in the poetry section, and went to talk to the librarian at the issue desk. He picked a book at random – a new one by the look of the unblemished cover. It was a collection of poems by a fellow called Siegfried Sassoon.

John had never heard of him and started to read. He realised at once they were about the war but he steeled himself and read on. One in particular caught his eye, talking about the hell where youth and laughter go. That set something off in him, and he bent his head and cried silent tears. He hoped no one would notice but after a few moments he felt a hand on his shoulder and looked up. It was one of the library assistants – that girl with curly red hair who always smiled at him. Everyone else in that section of the library had moved away from him. She patted him on the shoulder and left him to his tears.

Gathering his thoughts, he put the book back on the shelf, telling himself he would never read a poem like that again. But ten minutes later, his curiosity got the better of him. He went back and took the book down once more and went over to the issue desk.

On the way back to the hospital, Annie linked her arm around his and they talked about the books they had read and he told her he didn't usually read poetry.

They were both startled by a street photographer who insisted on taking a picture. 'You look like a lovely couple,' he said.

John blushed and was about to say that actually they weren't a couple of all. But Annie just laughed and said 'When will the picture be ready? I think I'll have two copies.' She left her address at the hospital. 'I'll pay for it,' she said breezily.

When Annie took him back to the hospital he sat by the fire in the day room and read the Sassoon poems from start to finish. They made him weep with bitterness and regret. When Nurse Stamp came in she took the book away from him and told him he should not be reading material that caused him to behave in such a cowardly and unmanly way. He no longer cared what she thought – Annie wouldn't have said that to him.

Afterwards he felt better. Like a weight had been lifted from his shoulders. That night he dreamed about Harry again and when Annie woke him up he had a clear memory of what had happened. He was calling to someone he knew very well, calling to them to keep down and catch up. And then they had been caught by shrapnel...Harry, it was. That name was so familiar to him, but he couldn't place it. He could feel the knowledge of it pressing like a great weight of water. Maybe it would come to him if he let it...

Preston
20th November 1920
Lizzie Kirke was always pleased to get a letter from her friend Annie Scott. She envied her sometimes, living in London. She thought she ought to try and get a job down there again, while she was still young... Maybe she'd find a nice young man. There were few enough now here in Preston. The war had hit the town particularly hard.

Annie had sent her a photograph of one of her patients. The one who'd lost his memory. The one they called John. She'd written to Lizzie about him before, telling her what a nice man he was, and handsome too, despite the scar on his forehead. Annie was obviously fascinated by him, and probably a bit closer to him than professional decorum permitted. But Lizzie didn't care about that. They'd all suffered in the war. The men most of all, but the women too. Everyone she knew had lost someone close. She looked at the photo again, after she had read the letter, and recognition dawned. That face. This John looked a lot like Edie Spencer's boy Albert. She remembered him from church. She hadn't seen him for a few years now, but it could almost be him.

She thought of Edie and Tom Spencer, but couldn't bring herself to show them the photo. There had been an incident with another mother she knew a few weeks before, with a picture in the paper. It hadn't been her dead boy, after all. Lizzie didn't want to do that to Edie. It would be too painful.

Edie and Tom had lost both their boys within a day or two. And right at the end of the war. The telegrams had arrived barely a week before it ended. Harry was buried out there in the Somme. Edie and Tom had visited the grave just this summer. But Albert had gone missing. They thought he'd been blown to pieces, or maybe buried alive by a shell. Edie was telling her just the other day how they were sure it was him in the coffin, when they buried the Unknown Soldier at Westminster Abbey.

Lizzie put Annie's letter in the shoebox she used to keep her correspondence and began to draft a reply:

Your soldier friend looks very like a boy I knew from church: Albert Spencer. I work with his mum sometimes, at the retreat for invalid soldiers. Poor woman lost both her boys. She had the telegrams about Albert and his brother Harry in the same week. They never found Albert so I suppose he's still out there in the mud. But maybe you ought to ask your friend if he has a brother? You never know what he might remember...

EDITOR'S NOTE

It might help to increase your appreciation of the stories in this collection if you know a little more about the First World War...

The First World War began in August 1914 and ended on November 11th 1918, and was the result of years of tension and competition between the 'great powers' of Europe, most of which thought of themselves as empires – Britain, France and Russia on one side, Germany, Austria-Hungary and Italy on the other. To begin with it was a war of movement, with Germany attacking France through Belgium and Luxembourg. But modern weapons such as machine guns and heavy artillery were so devastating in the open that the armies soon 'dug in'. So from the autumn of 1914 until the war ended in 1918, the 'Western Front', which spanned and both Belgium and northern France, was almost entirely made up of armies in lines of trenches, that faced each other, and ran from Switzerland to the English Channel.

That's usually the image that comes to mind when we think of the First World War, and it was a terrible conflict. Millions of men died from artillery bombardments and in frontal attacks where they were mown down by machine guns. It was the first properly 'industrial' war, and science was used to develop even more terrible weapons, such as poison gas. Planes were used too, and later in the war the first tanks were deployed to break through the line of trenches. There were an enormous number of casualties in some battles – on July 1st 1916, for example, the first day of the Battle of the Somme – 30,000 soldiers were killed and many more were wounded.

There was plenty of fighting elsewhere, though, with major campaigns in Italy, against Turkey on the Gallipoli peninsula, in the Middle East, and in Africa, where most of the European powers had colonial possessions. There were naval battles too, the most famous being the Battle of Jutland in the North Sea, where the British and German fleets fought each other and both claimed victory. Submarines were also used for the first time – Germany using them to attack merchant shipping in the Atlantic – famously sinking the *Lusitania*, a passenger liner. Air raids were another first – Germany sent its 'Zeppelin' airships to bomb London and other British targets.

EDITOR'S NOTE

There was a great deal of fighting in south-eastern Europe and the Balkans, and a vast campaign in which Germany defeated Russia.

By the time the war was over, nine million soldiers had died, 21 million were wounded, and many of the survivors were mentally scarred for the rest of their lives with what we now call 'post-traumatic stress disorder' or PTSD, but which was known at the time as 'shell shock'.

The countries that fought in the war were changed forever too. In Russia, the Tsar was deposed (and eventually killed with his family), in a communist revolution. The German Kaiser abdicated, and Germany was punished by the victorious allies, something which caused huge bitterness and resentment among the German people. Fifteen years later Adolf Hitler, leader of the Nazi party, swept to power and set Germany on a path that would lead to the Second World War in 1939, which many people saw as merely a continuation of the 'unfinished business' of 1914–1918.

Of course, there have been many books about the First World War (or 'The Great War' as it was known until 1939), both histories and fiction. I would recommend *World War One – A Short History* by Norman Stone, and *The Great War and Modern Memory* by Paul Fussell, as well as any books by an excellent British historian of the conflict; Lyn Macdonald. The war also produced a number of great poets, men like Isaac Rosenberg and Wilfred Owen, both of whom were killed; Siegfried Sassoon, Robert Graves and Edmund Blunden, who all wrote memoirs of their time in the trenches. Their work is certainly worth reading. I would also recommend Michael Morpurgo's *War Horse* and *Private Peaceful*, Michael Foreman's *War Game*, and Theresa Breslin's *Remembrance*.

Last but not least, there are several websites worth exploring too, in particular those of The Imperial War Museum at www.iwm.org.uk/centenary; The National Archives at www.nationalarchives.gov.uk/pathways/firstworldwar/; and the BBC at www.bbc.co.uk/history/worldwars/wwone/.

Tony Bradman

A Note on the Contributors

Jamila Gavin has been publishing stories, novels and plays for children aged six to sixteen for the last thirty years. Shortlisted for the Smarties Award, the Carnegie Medal and the Guardian Children's Fiction Award, for which she was also runner up with *The Wheel of Surya*, she won the Whitbread Children's Book Award in 2000 with *Coram Boy*, which was later adapted for the stage by Helen Edmundson for the National Theatre in London, and after two successful runs transferred to New York. Other novels for young adults include *The Blood Stone* and *The Robber Baron's Daughter*. Recent publications have been *Tales from India*, *School for Princes* and *Alexander the Great: Man, Myth or Monster*. Her latest book, published November 2013 is *Blackberry Blue and other Fairytales* – written in the European tradition, they reflect the diversity of the new multicultural Europeans of today.

Ian Beck is the author and illustrator of many picture books for children. He has also written several novels and short stories, including *The Secret History of Tom Trueheart*, which has been translated into over twenty languages.

Nigel Hinton is the author of over twenty books and has also written screenplays for TV and movies. He loves films, reading, football, music, drawing and painting, and walking along the sea. He plays guitar (badly) and ukulele (a bit better) and writes songs, some of which have been recorded.

Tim Bowler has written over twenty books for teenagers and won fifteen awards, including the Carnegie Medal for *River Boy*. He has been described by the *Sunday Telegraph* as 'the master of the psychological thriller' and by the *Independent* as 'one of the truly individual voices in British teenage fiction'. His works include *Starseeker*, *Apocalypse*, *Frozen Fire*, *Bloodchild*, *Buried Thunder*, *Sea of Whispers* and the *BLADE* series. His new novel *Night Runner* is due out in August 2014.

Linda Newbery has written for young readers of all ages, and won the Costa Children's Book Prize for her young adult novel *Set in Stone*. Other titles include *The Sandfather*, *Catcall*, *The Treasure House*, *Nevermore* and *At the Firefly Gate*. Her most recent publication is a short, dyslexia-friendly novel of the First World War, *Tilly's Promise*, published by Barrington Stoke. *The Shell House* (shortlisted for the Carnegie Medal) is a mystery set partly in the present and partly in 1916–1917, and is reissued this year. She lives in a small Oxfordshire village with her husband, two cats and three chickens.

Malorie Blackman has written over sixty books including the *Noughts and Crosses* series of novels, *Cloud Busting*, *Hacker* and *Boys Don't Cry*. In 2008, Malorie was honoured with an OBE for her services to Children's Literature, and in June 2013, she was appointed Children's Laureate 2013–2015.

Adele Geras is the author of almost 100 books. Her novel *Troy* was shortlisted for both the Carnegie Medal and the Whitbread (now Costa) Award. In the USA, she won the Sidney Taylor Award and the National Jewish Book Award for *My Grandmother's Stories*. A picture book called *It's Time For Bed* illustrated by Sophy Williams was published in 2012 and a novel for adults, *Cover Your Eyes*, is coming from Quercus in 2014. She lives in Cambridge and has two daughters and three grandchildren.

Oisin McGann grew up in Dublin and Drogheda in Ireland. He has written and illustrated numerous books for children and young adults, including the *Mad Grandad* series, *The Forbidden Files* series and his latest novel, the sci-fi crime thriller, *Rat Runners*.

Geraldine McCaughrean has written more books than she can name and had more joy doing so than is quite allowed. Her awards include the Carnegie Medal, Whitbread, Smarties, Blue Peter and Printz. From picture books to adult novels, from plays and short stories, to poems and retellings, no unwritten story can hope to escape for long the sharp point of her pen. Geraldine is best known for her sequel to Peter Pan, *Peter Pan in Scarlet*, in which the guns of the First World War have damaged the fabric of Neverland. If you enjoy her story here, you might well enjoy *Tamburlaine's Elephants*, *The Kite Rider*, *Plundering Paradise* and *101 Stories from British History*.

Sophie Masson was born in Indonesia of French parents, and brought up in Australia and France. She is the author of more than fifty novels for children, young adults and adults, published in Australia and many other countries, including the UK. Her historical novel, *The Hunt for Ned Kelly* (Scholastic Australia), won the prestigious Patricia Wrightson Prize for Children's Literature in the 2011 NSW Premier's Literary Awards, and many of her books have been shortlisted for other awards. Her most recent books are the YA fairytale novel *Scarlet in the Snow* (Random House Australia), the picture book *Two Trickster Tales from Russia* (Christmas Press, Australia 2013) and, under the pen-name of Jenna Austen, *The Romance Diaries: Stella* (Harper Collins Australia 2013), for tween and teen readers. Her second novel about the Great War, titled *1914*, comes out with Scholastic Australia in 2014.

Leslie Wilson had an English father and a German mother and was brought up bilingual. She is the author of two novels for young people about Nazi Germany: *Last Train from Kummersdorf* and *Saving Rafael.*

Paul Dowswell writes historical fiction for children. His last two novels, *Sektion 20*, set in communist East Berlin, and *Eleven Eleven*, set on the final day of the Great War, have both won the Historical Association Young Quills Award.

A NOTE ON THE EDITOR

Tony Bradman has been involved in the world of children's books for more than 30 years, as an award-winning writer, an editor and a reviewer. He has written books for all ages – poetry, picture books and fiction – and has edited many anthologies of short stories and poetry. In recent years he has also written a number of books with his son Tom, including *Titanic: Death in the Water* which won a Young Quills Award from the Historical Association in 2012.